HOW TO *Salsa* IN A SARI

Dona Sarkar

HOW TO *Salsa* IN A SARI

KIMANI
TRU
TM

HOW TO SALSA IN A SARI

ISBN-13: 978-0-373-83088-6
ISBN-10:   0-373-83088-2

© 2008 by Dona Sarkar-Mishra

www.kimaniTRU.com

Printed in U.S.A.

To my mother, for always having a book on her nightstand and to Manav, my darling husband, for always making sure I have the same.

Acknowledgment

First of all, to my wonderful, supportive agent
Sha-Shana Crichton. Girl, YOU ROCK! You never
lost sight of my work and always, always believed I could
do it. You are truly more than an agent, you're my rock in this
whirlwind publishing industry and I can't say it enough.

To the whole Harlequin team: Evette, Glenda, Linda and crew.
Thanks for this amazing opportunity. You've truly made my
dreams come true.

To Nadine Dajani, thank you for giving me this amazing title and
teaching me more about lyrical prose and honest characters
than I could ever have learned in class or books. Your writing
encourages me to reach for more in every single sentence.

Heather Davis, when you read this book, you said, "This is the
one." I never forgot those words and I will never forget how you
took me under your wing and made me the confident person
I am today. You are truly one of the kindest, most loyal,
most beautiful people I have ever met and I am so blessed to
have you as my number-one critique partner.

To my Buzz Girls: With a support group like you, who needs
anything else. Bee fabulous!

To Janet Lee Carey and Gordon Donnell. Without you two,
this book, or Dona Sarkar the writer, wouldn't exist. Thanks for
taking the scared girl who walked into class that day in 2003
(who couldn't write a complete sentence) and making her
into a published author. You both are the writers
I admire most in the world. Thank you for always being
there and always being honest.

To all my friends from work, thanks for being with me on
this journey. You have no idea how much it meant to me every
time you asked, "Is your book out yet? Can we read it yet?"
Thank you.

To Krish and Nabhan. We've been together for ten years now and I can't tell you what your friendship means to me. You always told me I would become more than just a EECS graduate and you never stopped believing in me. I love you guys so much.

My family and friends around the world. Thanks for always being there for me and supporting my crazy ideas.

My Seattle posse: Your love and support during these past few years while I've gone from one low to another high has just been incredible. See you at the party!

Mummy and Papa, you took me into your home as your own daughter and brought me up to be what I am today. I was sitting in your living room when the phone rang and you were the first to hug me and tell me, "Of course you could do it!"

Minal and Nisarga. You guys are wonderful, supportive and everything siblings should be and I love you both so much. Enough said.

My mom and dad: You both raised me to be strong, independent and never stop chasing my dreams. You always told me I could do anything I put my mind to and I should know it. You were supportive from day one and I can never say enough how much it means to know I can pick up the phone and call you at any hour of the day.

My sister, Bonnie: Thanks for being my mole in the land of teenagers…and for always being ready to proofread a draft of anything I churn out. You were one of the first to read this book and you told me, "It's good. It's like, REALLY good." I'll never forget that.

And last, but MOST importantly, my husband, Manav. When I don't feel like writing, you pack me and my laptop into the car and drag me to the coffee shop. When I'm down, you hold me as I cry and when I'm happy, you start the celebrations. You were with me the day I got "the call" and you were the only one not surprised. Thank you for knowing I could do it and convincing me of that fact when I lost faith. You're beyond a best friend or a husband. You are truly the other half of my being and because of you, I live with the most incredible feeling in the world, knowing I have you and Ash, my two precious guys, to come home to every single day.

CHAPTER 1

Life's Tough. Get a Helmet!

"Your life is going to change forever tonight, so be ready."

Issa Mazumder stopped in her tracks at her mother's mystifying phrase. "Mom!" she protested. Still clad in Power Puff Girl pajamas, not to mention sans coffee, Issa was in no shape for guessing games. "You are not messing with me right now!"

"I won't say another word. I was going to wait till the weekend, but today seems like a good day. It's a surprise."

Issa dropped into the chair opposite her mother and prepared her best wide-eyed "look how cute I am" expression. Nothing she loved more than one of Alisha Mazumder's surprises.

Just last month she and Alisha had made an impromptu trip to Manhattan when the Cirque de Soliel had come to the city. They had worked as ushers and seen the show for free from the front row.

"I'll die! I'm not even kidding. Physically die!"

"I'll pick you up here at six. Be ready!" Alisha

Mazumder raised an eyebrow over a steaming coconut latte. "I don't think you'll physically die."

"I can't think of anything else now. How could you do this to me?"

"This is quite the change from the panic-stricken daughter who was totally freaking last night about some exam." Alisha laughed. "What happened to 'Oh my God, I'm totally going to fail the World Politics midterm. My life means nothing beyond this exam!'"

"Whatever. I'm never panicked. Steady as a train. See that?" Issa flexed her puny biceps. "And quit changing the subject."

"Steady like a train wreck." Alisha grinned. "Talked to Adam finally?"

"Yup." Issa had to smile. She supposed the subject could turn to Adam. For a few seconds anyway.

Anxious, adorable Adam. Her boyfriend of two years had called at midnight with a panic attack of his own. He needed help. He needed support. More than anything…he needed her notes.

And if anything could make Issa feel better, it was fixing a problem. She'd drilled the study material into Adam's head and realized that she knew her stuff pretty well in comparison to her first and only love.

"He hadn't studied for the exam at all. His ass was set up to fail," Issa said as she got up to fill a mug with soy milk and pop it into the microwave. The Mazumder family ritual of spending a half hour every morning discussing school, work, cute boys, etc., over coconut lattes was Issa's favorite part of the day. Often, she felt it was the only time she and her mother could completely and totally be themselves, fuzzy pajamas and bed-head included. Over the years, she'd come to savor these last few minutes of dreamy innocence before the Mazumder girls donned protective shields and journeyed into the perilous world of high school.

"So, if Adam wasn't studying, what was Nerd Boy doing all weekend?" Alisha folded a corner in her *Modern Art and Design* magazine, buffed nails gleaming as she flipped the pages. "Shooting up? Loose women, fast cars?"

"Ha-ha." Issa made a face. She retrieved the steaming mug of milk from the microwave after the insistent beep. "He was sick, remember? He called me yesterday and told me he was on bed rest all day Friday and Saturday. Do you need to be calling him Nerd Boy all the time?"

"Uh, yeah. Otherwise, why would he date you?" Alisha teased, swirling her coffee cup. "Nerd Girl!"

"Hey!" Issa glanced up from where she was adding co-conut syrup and two shots of espresso into her monster-sized latte. "I protest!"

"Mommy, Mommy, I'm going to fail school. Will you still love me? Will you support me if I don't get into any college and have to live in a two-story cardboard box on the driveway?" Alisha mimicked Issa's paranoid ramblings from last night. "I swear, if I'd studied half as much as you do I would have been the mayor by now."

"You could be a rocket scientist, Mama." Alisha was an enigma to Issa. An eternally glamorous, bohemian version of Catherine Zeta-Jones, Alisha looked ten years younger than her thirty-six years and was one of the most dynamic people Issa knew. Everyone who met Alisha was in love with her wit, charm and vivacious personality within ten minutes.

"Thanks for your concern, my love." Alisha stood and shook the cheese Danish crumbs off her tiered blue velvet skirt. "You need a ride to school?"

Issa had to call Adam one last time to make sure he wasn't panicking, but refused to confess that to her mother and risk more teasing. "I'll walk, actually. Clear my head. Make sure I have all the world politics straight."

"Again, I repeat. Nerd!" Alisha called as she waltzed up the stairs. "Where do you get it from?"

Issa caught sight of Alisha's half-empty mug on the kitchen counter and almost laughed.

A total free spirit. No rules and regulations could keep Alisha in one place for long. While Issa envied Alisha's daydreamy attitude, she knew that one person in the house had to be somewhat responsible.

"I wonder too, Mama," Issa murmured, smiling as she rinsed out the cup and placed it into the dishwasher. Sometimes she swore her list-making obsession and punctuality existed to compensate for Alisha's short-term memory. Speaking of short-term memory, Alisha had managed to escape without revealing her surprise.

"Damn. She's good. She's really good," Issa grumbled as she grabbed a notepad off the kitchen counter. *So much to do today,* she thought. *One, drop off article at* Apex.

She wrote for the school newspaper as part of her writing scholarship at the prestigious private school. She worked hard on all her articles for the *Athens Apex* knowing Alisha would never be able to afford to send her to the hoity-toity school without the scholarship.

Last night, Issa had just finished up an investigative article on Thomas Calabran, one of the reclusive oil tycoons in town, three days before the deadline. Even she had to admit the article was one of her better works.

"Hey, your aunt Helen called," Alisha yelled over the sound of her hair dryer upstairs. "She wants to know if you want to do Kwanzaa in Atlanta again this year. Call her back, would you?"

Strict Aunt Helena. Her father's oldest sister had never approved of the mixed-race marriage of her Indian mother and African-American father. But she loved Issa like her own child and insisted Issa "keep her black flavor ripe." Issa had celebrated the African holiday during the last week of December with her father's family every year since she was a kid. Despite her father's absentee status, it was the one holiday she looked forward to, just to be able to see her extended family. The black, red and green decorations, the homegrown fruits, beautiful objects of art…she loved it all. The weeklong celebration made her feel like a part of her father's culture. A part she felt like she barely got to experience in the preppy, white-bread Connecticut town they had moved to at the beginning of high school.

"I'll call her, Mom. Please just finish doing your hair. You don't want to frizz."

"Aye-aye, Capitane."

Issa smiled and returned to her list.

Two, talk to Professor Kidlinger about the independent-study project.

English was the class she excelled at without trying and her teacher, Ms. Kidlinger, was always telling her she would accomplish great things with her talent for words. Issa had come up with a master plan to ask her teacher if she could do an independent-study project on Jane Austen and her life during the *Pride and Prejudice* era next semester.

Three...

"Hey!" Alisha called again, snapping Issa out of her list. "Cute-boy-on-the-patio alert!"

Issa's pen hit the counter a second before the knock on the kitchen door. "Are those cheese Danishes I smell?"

Adam.

"Hey!" Issa threw open the door and greeted the smiling junior with a big kiss. "I didn't expect to see you this morning."

Her Adam. Buttery ribbons of blond hair, eyes that twinkled like Christmas lights and the most innocent smile Issa had ever seen. So he wasn't traditionally gorgeous with his mild sprinkling of acne and too-thin frame, but Issa found him adorable and perfect for her.

Adam's lightly freckled face crinkled even more around the eyes than usual. "Hello, gorgeous."

Issa's cheeks burned. Adam always claimed she looked like the girl from *Bend It Like Beckham,* but she didn't believe it for a second. Alisha was the great beauty in the family, Issa was just a mess of tangled, murky brown hair and tennis-ball-sized, anxious eyes. Their homecoming pictures had been beautiful, though, his cream complementing her cocoa.

"How're you feeling? Better?" Issa stuffed a Danish into his hand.

"Listen, I need to run to an early morning Science Club

meeting, but I wanted to bring you this." From behind his back appeared a single lavender rose, Issa's favorite. "Thanks so much for helping me last night."

"You didn't have to." Issa took the flower and inhaled.

"I did have to," Adam said, encircling his hands around her back, pulling her head under his chin. Issa breathed in his CK aftershave as she leaned on him.

"Thanks so much, Iz. You're amazing." He kissed her nose. "Now I really need to go. I'll see you in class."

"Love you!" Issa called to him as he jogged down the driveway. He held up an arm without turning around.

She smiled and twirled on her bare feet. Adam was happy again. Problem solved.

After the last period of the day, the World Politics exam successfully behind her, Issa left the school newspaper office where her article was safely nesting in the editor's layout box. She sped through the halls, having gotten a text message from Gigi five minutes earlier.

EMERGENCY! I NEED TO SEE YOU! CHEM LAB! NOW!

Issa flew around a corner and skidded on the freshly waxed floor, her Sketchers screeching to a stop.

Latina Barbie and the Skipper twins, combined weight and IQ of 100, stood blocking the hallway.

"Well, well." Cat Morena, aka Latina Barbie, crossed her arms, a smirk in her slanted green eyes. "If it isn't the affirmative-action case." She emphasized the word with an extra *S* at the end. She covered her slight Cuban accent with a faux British one. "Off to help Mummy scrub the floors to earn your keep?"

Issa clenched her teeth. Rudeness on a daily basis was expected from Cat, but she was dissing Alisha now, the best art teacher Athens Academy had ever had. How low could Cat really go?

However, Issa kept quiet. She'd learned long ago that Cat *wanted* her to fight back. A cross between a dark-haired Paris Hilton and an even darker poisonous viper, Cat liked nothing better than to put one of her enemies in their place. Issa remembered well the first time she had challenged Cat. The first and last time she'd crossed Cat Morena.

"I got somewhere to be," Issa muttered, rubbing her toe against the sparkling floor.

"So, what do you want us to do about it, huh, *chica?*"

Issa could see the reflection of Cat and her entourage on the floor as Cat tossed her perfectly highlighted caramel-colored hair and smiled snidely, waiting for some sort of response from Issa.

"No answer? Are you going to run to Mommy and tell her we're being mean to you? Are you going to cry?" Cat's singsong voice could cut sharper than any knife. "Are you wishing we would leave you alone?"

For a moment, Issa felt like she might actually cry. She didn't understand why Cat was so mean. So they'd had a fight over two years ago. She had no idea how Cat could hold a grudge for so long. How a privileged sixteen-year-old girl could be so deliberately cruel to someone was beyond Issa.

"I don't have time for this bullshit right here," Issa finally snapped, her voice betraying her bravado with a quaver. Damn it. Issa never liked giving Cat the satisfaction of knowing how to get to her. Like a vampire feeding off blood, Cat fed off people's weaknesses.

One of the blond Skipper twins, Jewel Taylor, giggled. "Aw, how cute. She's using her black talk. What's it called, Sunshine?"

"Ebonics! That's what it's called!" The other twin, Sunshine Harris, joined in the giggling.

Issa's cheeks burned. As one of the few biracial students in the school, she made sure to avoid sounding "black" for just this reason. Anything that wasn't "Like, oh my God," was "black talk" to the masses of rich white folks. Even her schoolteacher father would *never* have stood for Ebonics in his house.

Cat stopped laughing, an unpredictable look in her eyes. "Fine. Go," she said quietly. "Your day's about a get a whole lot worse, *chica.*"

Shit.

A needle of fear jabbed Issa as she ran through the hallways. Cat hadn't spent as much time torturing her as usual. As Issa well knew, that was never a good thing. She had learned that lesson the first semester of her freshman year.

Issa had made it a point to avoid Cat at all costs for the next year and a half. And succeeded. She and Cat traveled in totally different circles. Cat was always surrounded by her perfumed, feathered, rich friends and Issa hung with down-to-earth, out-of-place types.

Only a few months ago had Cat come back into Issa's life, now that they were both enrolled for the same English class. Issa made it a point to sit in the far back of the room, huddled into oversized sweatshirts in the corner, trying to be as invisible as possible.

Issa shivered, remembering Cat's words. By the time she reached the chemistry lab, she had a very bad case of dread squeezing at her stomach.

"Gigi! What's the emergency, girl?" Issa spotted her friend hunched over an array of tubes and beakers.

Gigi O'Neil held up a test tube filled with a suspiciously slimly green liquid. "Does this look right? Mr. Jonas said if I don't finish this lab by the end of the day, I'm totally failing the class."

"Gigi—"

"I think I just made a bomb!"

"Gigi!"

"Wait, let me put the bomb down. I don't want to blow us up before you hear the news."

Gigi set her bomb carefully into a beaker. She nervously pushed her goggles to the top of her wavy red hair and blinked her aquamarine eyes. "Just so you know, I could be wrong. If I'm right, I don't want you to hate me. I just thought you should know. Okay? So promise not to hate me?"

Issa restrained the urge to reach out and wrap her hands around Gigi's throat. It figured, her friend had to be a ditz at a moment like this.

"Girl, do not mess with me right now!" Issa snapped, curiosity building to the point of annoyance. Even though Gigi was often theatrical, this didn't sound like the usual round of stupid Monday-morning gossip.

"So, remember you said Adam was sick on Friday night

and that was why he couldn't come see the movie with us and Ishaan?"

Issa nodded.

"There you guys are." Ishaan Banerjee stormed the door of the lab, his handsome face not looking a least bit pleased. His heavy black eyebrows were drawn together in a fierce V and his usually full mouth was set in a horizontal line. "Gigi, did you tell her? I swear, I'm gonna kill that guy."

His fists were clenched and he looked ready to do some damage.

Ishaan was intense and passionate, but hardly violent. Something had brought out his protective edge. Issa wished someone would just tell her what the hell was going on. How was she always the last to know the news?

"Guys. What's going on?" Issa looked at her two closest friends. They each hesitated as they exchanged a look. "Is it that bad? Am I being kicked out of school?"

"Well," Gigi started, "Matt told Ishaan he saw Adam at Cat Morena's house on Friday night. For one of her hot-tub parties."

Issa's breath caught. Adam? No way. That was stupid. He'd been even sweeter than usual this morning. Adam would never do anything like this. He loved her and thought Cat and her friends were useless flakes.

"Future barefoot and pregnant housewives, Issa, that's all they are," he always said to her. "They're jealous of you and your real future."

This had to be some stupid rumor. Maybe there was someone who looked like Adam making the rounds. There had to be some other explanation.

Issa breathed a sigh of relief. Jeez, she expected these theatrics from Gigi, but Ishaan? He never repeated news from the Athena Gossip Mill.

That is, unless he knew it to be true.

No, not possible.

"I don't think so, guys. I mean, we know Adam. I think we're all just overreacting." She forced a smile for her friends. What if it *was* true?

"That's not the worst part." Ishaan cut her off. "Iz, *apparently* Adam was doing Jell-O shots off of Cat Morena's neck."

"What!"

Suddenly Cat's words came back to Issa.

Your day's about to get a whole lot worse, chica.

This had to be what that horrible witch had meant.

"She's hyperventilating. Get a chair," Gigi ordered Ishaan.

"I am not—" Before she knew what was happening, Ishaan had grabbed a plastic chair that caught Issa's weight just before her knees gave out. "I am not—"

Adam? Party? Cat Morena's neck?

Issa counted to ten and hoped she was dreaming. "But— Oh. I feel dizzy."

She replayed the events of the weekend over in her head. Adam calling her at 8:00 p.m. on Friday night to tell her he wasn't feeling too hot and wouldn't be able to join them at the movies. Did he sound sick then? Her mind was too foggy to remember. But then, after she'd gotten home, she'd dialed his cell phone to check on him. He hadn't answered.

But he was sick! He was probably asleep, nitwit, her mind argued back.

"Okay, guys, let's think about this. Like logically." Gigi

interrupted her thoughts. "Ishaan got this news from the Athens Gossip Mill. Maybe it's a miscommunication type of thing. You know what happens when couples don't communicate, right? Remember in the O.C. when Marissa didn't tell Ryan about Trey attacking her? Then Ryan thought they were doing it and he got so pissed and—"

"Bottom line, Iz. Is this something Adam would do?" Ishaan, thankfully, cut Gigi off. "If it's true, I'll kill him." Ishaan rolled up the sleeves of his button-down and slammed his left fist into his right hand. "He's dead. What would he want with that psycho bitch?"

Well, Issa knew what Adam would want from Cat. What every other guy in school wanted. Cat wasn't called "La Cuerpa" for no reason. If this rumor was even true, that is.

The real question was what Cat wanted with *Adam*. It wasn't enough that Cat had already had the Homecoming Princess title, an accent guys were gaga over, more money than Britney Spears could dream of and a body every girl in school would give up their trust funds for. But now she wanted Adam Mitchell? Nerdy, band-geek Adam.

Not possible.

This rumor was getting too stupid to even make the rounds. Issa was going to put an end to it immediately.

"I need to talk to him. He'll tell me the truth." Issa stood up.

Ishaan muttered something and Gigi gave him a sharp look. "That's a good idea, Iz. I mean, if he wasn't there, then…"

Issa stopped listening. Adam! She saw his familiar silhouette close a locker door and pile his books up high in the hallway.

"There he is! Gotta go." She dashed out of the classroom and into the crowded hallway. Her friends were still standing in the chem lab, concerned expressions on their faces.

Adam was going to be so pissed when he heard the rumor. Maybe it was time the two of them confronted Cat and told her to go to hell once and for all.

"Hey." Issa wrapped her arms around Adam's bony back, ignoring her usual "no PDA" rule. It felt so good to hold him after her horrendous afternoon.

"Issa, hey. Uh, what's up?" He gave her a strange smile and pushed his tortoiseshell glasses up his nose.

"Argh." She slipped her hand into his. "I had a crazy afternoon. What about you? How was the test? Do you feel better?"

"Yeah. Much."

"Are you all recovered from your cold?"

"Uh, yeah. I got a lot of rest over the weekend, so…"

There it was. Adam probably lay around the whole weekend in his room nursing his cold and missing her. She should have stopped by. Poor baby.

Issa sidestepped a gothic freshman couple making out against the lockers and glanced away enviously. She and Adam used to be like that. Of course, not in a public hallway for the whole school to see, but they had gotten pretty hot and heavy in Adam's car after Homecoming earlier that year—till they were interrupted so rudely by passing headlights anyway. Issa smiled. That had been a good night. She couldn't wait till Prom to complete what they had started that night.…

Lately, school had gotten so busy she felt like they'd started to take each other for granted. Felt like the only thing they got together to do anymore was study—actually study—not sneak kisses while Adam's mom was downstairs.

Issa sighed. They had to get back to being crazy and in love again. Like that morning. It had been ages since Adam had surprised her with flowers. She needed to just be honest with Adam and confess what was bothering her. It was the first step.

"Hey, listen. Thought you should know." Issa hesitated. Should she even tell him? Oh, why not? They would get a good laugh about it and she could finally put it behind her. "There's this weird rumor going on about you and Cat Morena, and I, uh, wanted to ask you about it."

She expected Adam to laugh and tell her he would never have anything to do with a ditz like Cat. Instead, he frowned.

"Iz, I really needed to talk to you about something on Friday, but I didn't get the chance."

Why didn't he deny the rumor?

"Oh…okay." Issa stopped. She wasn't sure she liked his tone.

"Hey, Adam." A group of guys with broad football-player shoulders came by and clapped Adam on the back. "Going to Sunshine's party this weekend?"

"Uh, yeah…" The freckles popped out on Adam's nose. He nervously ran his fingers through his dirty blond hair.

The football-player crowd was actually taking the time to talk to Adam. Not to mention he was invited to one of

Sunshine's parties. Sunshine Harris, Queen of the Nasty Cheerleaders. Cat Morena's best friend, Skipper twin number two. No...this wasn't possible.

Issa watched as Adam made small talk with the jocks. What *did* he have in common with them? It certainly wasn't a love of academia.

Issa and Adam were at the top of their class, always competing for the coveted number-one spot that all Ivy League colleges looked at. They'd started off as study buddies during their freshman year and soon were spending every waking hour together, cramming biology and trigonometry into their heads, leaving no time for a social life. So when Adam had asked her to go to their freshman year Homecoming dance as his date, Issa was thrilled. With a roundish body, ragged hair and acne-prone skin, Issa knew she was no grand beauty and was happy just to be asked.

That was the night she realized that skinny, shy Adam cleaned up very nicely and her heart actually sped up when he held her in his arms for a slow dance. She wasn't surprised when he kissed her at her door that night. It just seemed so right.

And it had been that way for the past two years. Until now. Issa looked hard at her boyfriend. He was going to parties and not bothering to mention it to her. What next?

"So, uh, you're going to Sunshine's this weekend?" Issa felt the dread start to rise again as they walked away from the football players. "Were you at a party last weekend by any chance?"

Suddenly she didn't want to know. She wished she could

take the words back and live in her dreamworld for just a bit longer.

"Actually, that's what I wanted to talk to you about. Look." He stopped and pulled her into a quiet corner as a flood of band students paraded by with their tubas and trombones.

That's when Issa knew everything was about to change. Adam had been acting weird the past two weeks, but she had attributed his behavior to worrying about midterms.

"You're great, Iz, but sometimes I wonder why we're together. Don't you think that maybe, you know…"

"I don't know what you're trying to say. So I suggest you come right out and say it and quit stallin'." Her voice was growing high and she had an idea of what was going to happen next. This was Adam, *her* Adam. And he was breaking up with her. This couldn't be real. She felt like she was having an out-of-body experience.

Adam glanced around the hallway. A few people were staring at them. Issa realized the stricken look on her face was probably giving away what was going on in that corner. "I just need to find who I am. Before high school is over. I don't want to be this…nerd forever. I want to know who else I can become."

"What's wrong with who you are now?"

"I—we, ever since we started high school, we got into this routine and we've never tried anything new. Every day's the same. Classes, study dates, movies on Saturdays, debates. That's it. We can go through another two years of high school like this, or we can try something different."

Issa knew what he was trying to say, but she held on to

some hope. "So we'll both change. We'll go to football games, parties, all that stuff—"

"No. That wouldn't be different."

Everything was perfect. Cat Morena had once again swept into her life and turned everything inside out. Issa felt a burning hatred for Cat like she'd never felt before. "Different. You mean, me. You can just say it. You don't want me anymore."

"It's just that—I can't be with you and expect to change my life. It's always going to be the same and—"

"We're over," Issa stated in a steady voice, even though just saying the words shot a ten-pound stone into the center of her belly. "Who is she? Who is going to help you make over your life?"

"There's no one—"

Yeah, she knew very well who it was. "Cat Morena? You were doing Jell-O shots off of her neck as far as I hear."

"How did you—"

So it was true. He didn't even try to deny his lying and cheating.

"God, Adam. What the hell are you doing? The Cat Morenas of this world are only going to toy with you, then throw you away. She wants a modeling contract and some millionaire boyfriend to take care of her, not you!"

Adam was silent.

"Say something, you little freak!" Issa practically shrieked. Now everyone was openly staring at them, but she didn't care.

Before he could respond, a hush fell over the hallway as Cat and her cronies made their way through the crowd.

When the three of them spotted Issa and Adam, Cat turned her head and whispered something to Sunshine Harris. Then they both giggled while Cat shot Issa an evil smile.

"She's such a bitch. A horrible snake," Issa muttered, her fear of Cat evaporating. She didn't care anymore if Cat overheard. What did Issa have left to lose now?

Adam glanced away from Issa and toward the girls. He fidgeted with the strap of his backpack and untied one shoelace with his other foot. "Every guy wants her. And she likes me. She appreciates me, and she never tries to one-up me. Not like you."

Issa felt the tears start to well up in her eyes. That was what this whole thing was about? That was how he got seduced by Cat's charms? Because Cat made him feel *smart?* Cat could make a toadstool feel smart. This was not an accomplishment!

"I thought that was just a joke between us. I was just playin'. I thought all that 'top two people in class' was just for kicks."

Issa could feel her old downtown Detroit "don't take crap from anyone" attitude creeping in and she didn't give a damn. When she'd just moved to New Joliet, she'd gotten made fun of for being from "the ghetto" by all the popular girls. All they'd wanted to hear about was gang wars and shootings. No one had cared about the rich African-American heritage Detroit had produced or the incredible automotive industry that was housed in the city. She'd buried her past deep down and become the East Coast brainiac everyone expected her to be and never mentioned her roots again.

"Well, it wasn't fun for me," Adam said quietly. "I don't want a girlfriend who goes around telling everyone how much smarter she is than me. You may be smart, but that's all you are, Issa. Brains don't make a complete person!"

That did it. The tears started spilling from her eyes. She swiped her cheek with her shoulder. "Oh, my being smart didn't seem to bother you last night when you called crying in desperation!"

Adam didn't say anything. Apparently saving his ass in a moment of crisis wasn't as important as looking hot in a pair of Seven Jeans. Suddenly Issa felt like everything she knew about the world was wrong. Intelligent girls—zero. Slutty girls—ten points. "Forget it, you slimy little jackass. I hope you realize someday how much I appreciated you and how you'll never have that again."

Issa threw her head back and swept past Cat and her entourage with as much dignity as she could muster. She pretended not to hear their tinkling laughter behind her as she walked steadily into the girls' room. She was proud she'd been able to contain her sobbing until she was safely in the stall.

How could this be happening? They had just celebrated their two-year anniversary last week! The whole world knew they were together and how crazy she was about him. How could she go out in public and tell people that Adam had suddenly stopped loving her?

All Issa wanted was to go home. Hide in her bed until this nightmare ended. But by the sounds of lockers slamming shut and tennis shoes squeaking, she knew the hallways weren't clear yet. No, she couldn't get out of this hell until she was sure everyone was gone.

How would she ever be able to face Adam again with Cat Morena by his side?

CHAPTER 2

Men, Chocolate and Coffee Are All Better Rich

"I'm fine. Let's just stop talking about it, huh?" Issa, nestled into a mound of hand-embroidered pillows, glowered up at the ceiling. She knew if she met Ishaan's sad puppy eyes, she would burst into tears.

"Iz," Ishaan said, then reached over and tousled her ripply hair. "Do you want me to beat his ass? You know I will."

Tempting, but what good would it do? Adam would still be in love with Cat Morena and Issa would still be the laughingstock of the school. Cat had won again. Except this time, Issa didn't understand what she'd done to Cat and what Cat was really after. She refused to believe Cat had suddenly and painfully fallen in love with Adam Mitchell, the boy who in eighth grade was voted Most Likely to Host *Star Trek* Conventions in His Garage.

"Should I take that as a 'Yes, Ishaan, my hero, please beat up that jackass for me'?" Ishaan asked, his eyes twinkling.

Issa smiled despite the hideousness of the day. He always

knew how to make her feel better. "Don't beat his ass." She sighed. Ishaan played tennis and had a mean left hook. No matter how pissed she was at Adam at the moment, she didn't want him hurt.

"What reason did he give for ending it? And don't tell me he said it was because Cat was hotter than you."

Issa flinched. Well, pretty much that was exactly what he said. But she was ashamed to admit to Ishaan that her now ex-boyfriend found her to be intelligent yet repulsive to look at.

"He gave me some lame-ass reason about him being a nerd and me holding him back from being cool." She rolled her eyes as dramatically as she could. "Yeah, that was me all along. Anyway, it doesn't matter." Issa pushed Ishaan's hand away from her hair. "Let him do what he wants. He weighs ninety-five pounds, let's see if he can ever do anything *but* be a nerd."

The pink and purple saris Issa had hung on her windows shuddered gently in the breeze. Today, even hiding in the ethnic lair that was her bedroom wasn't comforting to her. The *Om*-printed jasmine candles and prints of the Taj Mahal and Jaipur on the walls weren't taking her away to another world like they usually did.

Let's see how soon Cat dumps him on his ass. She continued to glare at the ceiling.

After she and her mother had moved into this place, Issa had stood on a ladder, painted the ceiling navy blue and glued on glow-in-the dark moons. She'd thought they were the coolest things in the world and whenever she had friends over, she would turn off the lights to show off her mini solar system. Now they seemed like childish plastic blobs. *She* felt like a childish plastic blob.

"Is there anything I can do? Slash his tires? Get the soccer team together and paint 'male whore' on his garage door? Wouldn't that be a *Desperate Housewives* moment?"

Issa almost laughed at the thought. Even though Ishaan was one of the more popular members of the senior class and a star on the soccer and tennis teams, he was the most loyal friend she had. And usually she would tease him about his closeted *Desperate Housewives* addiction, but she didn't feel like it today. "There's no reason to do anything. I'm over it. He's a fool. Not spending another moment thinking about him. Okay? No more."

"You mean that?" To her annoyance, Ishaan sounded amused, and not a least bit convinced.

Issa sighed. Ishaan Banerjee knew her too well. His family was one of two other Indian families in New Joliet and the Banerjees had taken Alisha under their wing and acted as if the Mazumders were blood relatives, despite Issa's half-and-half status.

Alisha's parents and the Banerjees were from the same city of Calcutta in India. Even though Alisha didn't speak Bengali with Issa or her older brother, Amir, plus the fact that she was estranged from her superconservative parents, she still carried her heritage and encouraged her children to do the same.

And ever since Amir had moved to Los Angeles for school, Ishaan had taken it upon himself to look out for Issa as if she were his own little sister. Sometimes it drove her crazy, but today she was happy he'd insisted on coming over and sitting with her.

"Can we change the subject?" Issa asked. "I don't want to waste another moment on this. He deserves everything that's coming to him."

"Of course," Ishaan said. "You're completely over him, right?" he repeated. "Never going to think of him again."

"That's right."

"Good. Great. How about we—"

"Dumped for Cat Morena!" Issa burst out. "It had to be Cat Morena! The one person I can't stand on this whole earth! Girl thinks baklava comes out of volcanoes. So she drives a Lotus and wears those trashy four-inch-heeled boots that cost more than our mortgage. Is that really so great? You're a guy, Ishaan, do you think she's all that?"

"Uh—"

Issa hurried on, afraid to hear his answer. "And who invites every guy she dates over for a 'dip' in her dad's hot tub? She's a tramp!"

"But you're over him, remember?"

Issa gritted her teeth and stewed. She was over him. A smart girl like her was never again going to be hung up on some guy. She wasn't a typical moronic teenager and certainly wasn't going to start acting like one now. And if Adam was stupid enough to believe whatever Cat had told him, well, he definitely wasn't the Adam she had loved.

"I don't care what he does," she said. "I just always thought Adam would be too smart to fall for *those* kinds of girls." She realized she sounded petty, stupid…and jealous. But she had to let it all out. "Whatever. Let him have his fun. I give him a week before he comes crawling back. Then I'll be the one having fun. Hmm, how many ways can you say, 'Go to hell'? I'll tell him in other languages. Do we have an international thesaurus up in here?"

"Iz—" Ishaan was interrupted by the Maroon 5 ring tone of Issa's cell phone. She swore she saw a hint of a smile on his lips as he handed over the phone. "Here. I gotta go anyway. Gigi said she'd stop by and see you after cheer practice."

"Don't laugh at me!" she yelled as Ishaan left the room. "I'm over him. I hate him. If this is him, I'll give him a piece of my mind."

"It's your mom. She's picking you up for some surprise, remember?" Ishaan paused in her doorway. "Go out and have fun. This day can't get any worse, right?"

"This better be a good surprise, Mama," Issa said, sliding into the passenger side of Alisha's rust-colored Toyota Corolla. "I'm really not in the mood today."

Alisha tapped the steering wheel in tune to the radio, the silver bangles on her wrists jangling. "I think you'll like this one, oh, favorite daughter."

Hmph. Alisha's teasing. Never a care in the world for Alisha. Sometimes Issa swore she was the mother and Alisha the daughter. Times like this it annoyed her. Why couldn't she have a normal mother? One who fed her chicken soup and let her hide under the covers for a week.

"Whatever." Issa sighed and faced out the passenger-side window.

"Hey, kiddo, are you okay?" Alisha asked, turning Issa's chin toward her. "Have you been crying?"

Issa hesitated. Right now she just wanted to stop thinking about it. If Issa started on the pity party now, Alisha would be furious with Adam. She would threaten to kick his sorry ass. And the surprise would be ruined.

I'll tell her afterward, Issa decided. "No, I'm fine. Don't want to talk about it right now."

Alisha still looked concerned. "You sure, babe? We can do this later if you want."

"No, no. I—never mind. What's this surprise about? Are we going somewhere fancy?" Issa studied Alisha's outfit. She'd changed clothes after work. The starched blue blouse and gray pencil skirt her mother was wearing were a far cry from her usual floor-length skirts and peasant tops. Her normally wavy hair was straightened and pulled neatly back at the nape of her neck. Issa became aware she was in jeans and a ragged hoodie sweatshirt, her shoulder-length curls now in a messy bun. She was *not* dressed for a night out.

"You're dressed up! Are we finally going to see *Joseph and the Amazing Technicolor Dreamcoat?* Mom! I'm not dressed for the theater!"

"Issa, I can assure you with my strongest conviction that we would *not* be going to the theater on a Monday night." Alisha attempted to start the car. The engine huffed and shut off.

"Well, I never know with you." Issa was still suspicious. "Remember that time we took a bus to the Hamptons just to sell seashells by the seashore?"

"I was young and you were silly then," Alisha said, her crescent-shaped lips curving as the engine finally groaned to life.

"It was last year!"

"And wasn't it fun? A good surprise?"

"Yes," Issa admitted. Any adventure with Alisha at the helm was fun. She was not your usual conservative Indian-American mother. Raised by overly strict parents, she had run away from home, married someone handsome and inappropriate, had Issa and her brother soon after and never really grown up. Alisha had vowed years ago to raise Issa right, in a way her own parents had never done with her.

Issa and Alisha had always shared everything: size 6 clothes, the same hazel eyes, a taste for coconut lattes and sweet tea and secrets. Until today. Issa wondered what all the hush-hush was about. She watched the neighborhoods change from middle class to upper crust as the car whizzed through New Joliet.

Ten minutes later Alisha pulled into a circular driveway topped by a three-story mansion.

"What's this? Did we win the lottery? Is this our new house?"

Alisha laughed. "You'll see."

Issa had been joking, but Alisha's smile was so happy, for a second she thought it might be possible.

Alisha rang the doorbell with Issa hanging behind a few steps.

"*Buenas tardes,* Alisha." A formidable salt-and-pepper-haired man, fully suited down to polished loafers, answered the door in a slightly accented voice. "I'm so glad Issa was able to make it."

Diego.

Alisha had been casually dating the slick, overly polished man for a few months. Thankfully, Issa hadn't had too many run-ins with him. *He* was the surprise? This had to be his house. Alisha normally had fun taste in men, tormented artists who were consumed by their genius or wannabe comedians who considered the world their stage. True, the relationships never lasted more than a month, but Issa knew her mother was just enjoying life. It wasn't as if she was looking for her soul mate. Issa's daddy was still out there somewhere and she knew her mama could never be with anyone else for long.

But this Diego was different. Issa had heard he was rich, but apparently he was superrich. The expensive-looking suits, the fancy corporate-lawyer job, this vulgarly large house. So ridiculous. He looked like a clean-cut Antonio Banderas and sounded like him too. Not Alisha's style at all.

"I'm so glad you came tonight for dinner, Issa." Diego reached out to take Issa's zipped-up hoodie.

"Oh, yeah," she muttered, and shoved her fingers into her sweatshirt pockets. She wasn't about to reveal the ribbed Hindu-god-imprinted tank top she wore underneath.

"My young daughter will be joining us tonight. She is most anxious to meet you." Diego either ignored, or didn't understand, Issa's sullen attitude.

"Wonderful," Issa said through her teeth. Could this day really get much worse? She didn't know Diego's bratty kid and didn't particularly care to after the horrendous day she'd had.

She surreptitiously checked out the house as Diego hung up Alisha's coat. Wow. White marble everything. Spiral staircase, burgundy carpeting. It was like something out of a design magazine. And all of this for just Diego and his kid? It was a far cry from her and Alisha's run-down town house with mismatched garage-sale furniture.

A small movement caught Issa's eyes and she noticed a girl sauntering down the spiral staircase. A tiny smirk on her lips, the girl made her way to the base of the stairs, her narrow hips creating figure eights as she walked, her silky hair swishing around the waist of her white dress. Not just any girl. Cat Morena.

Issa heard a strange gurgling sound in her throat. Cat Morena was Diego's daughter? It couldn't be! Was she being "punked"?

The wicked smile Cat shot Issa assured her this was no dream. She was real. Deadly real.

"Catalina, meet Issa, Alisha's daughter. I am sure you two have seen each other at school, yes?" Diego kissed his daughter's outstretched hand.

"Of course, *Papi*. Issa and I have some common friends. Adam, right?" Cat said the words so sweetly, Issa almost believed the innocent tone herself. "We were just talking about her last weekend while studying."

Studying? Yeah, he was studying your a— "Girl, I think you were doing a lot more than studying!" Issa spat before she could stop herself.

"Issa!" Alisha looked shocked. "What on earth…"

Anger took over her words and Issa felt herself starting to lose control. "Adam and I broke up. And it's because of—"

"Adam was not good enough for you. Not to worry, *chica*. He'll get what he deserves," Cat said in a reassuring voice. "Alisha, tell your daughter. Those high-school boys, so fickle. One day they are yours, the next, going after someone prettier and more popular."

What the hell kind of game was she playing? How did she manage to make every insult sound like a compliment? "I—"

"We should sit," Diego interrupted, looking over at Alisha. Pity, he looked as if he had no idea of the kind of activities that went on up in his house.

Dip in the hot tub, anyone?

Issa seethed and remembered Cat's words this morning.

Off to help your mommy scrub the floors.

Oooh, when Alisha found out, Diego would get hell. That would put an end to this screwed-up relationship.

"It is such an honor to finally have you here for dinner, *Professora!*" Cat practically purred, taking Alisha's arm and leading her to the living room with Issa dragging her feet behind.

She was going to ignore Cat, get through this dinner and never speak to her mother again.

"Call me Alisha. Please." Alisha smiled at Cat, earning a scornful look from Issa.

Diego and Alisha sat next to each other on a white leather couch, with Cat taking the ottoman. That left the love seat on which Issa perched, trying to edge as far away from the Morenas as possible.

The leather couch was sticking to her pants. She gingerly pulled her low-rise jeans up, the squeaking noise attracting Cat's attention.

"Is that a tattoo?" Cat said in an overtly loud voice.

Knowing Cat, she was hoping Alisha didn't know and Issa would get busted for it.

Diego stopped talking and glanced over at Issa with a frown.

Issa quickly pulled her sweatshirt down over the *Om* tattoo on her hip. The previous year she'd been obsessed with Sanskrit, the ancient Indian language, and had half joked she would love to have the symbol of the whole universe tatooed on her to remind herself to keep her cool through the crazy teenage years. To her surprise, Alisha had agreed to let Issa get the tattoo on her sixteenth birthday and had even gotten one herself.

"Iz and I got matching ones." Alisha raised her blouse to show Cat her own tattoo. "Cool, huh?"

"Yeah." Cat looked awestruck.

Diego looked horrified.

Issa could feel herself smiling. Hopefully now Alisha would see how ill-fit she and Diego were. It was like Gwen Stefani dating Donald Trump.

Or maybe not. Diego resumed his serene smile and put his arm around Alisha as if he had no problem dating a woman who let her sixteen-year-old daughter permanently scar herself. "So, Catalina, Issa, how were your days at school today?"

Issa pointedly stared out the window in the living room at the darkened sky. Ugh, she could see Diego's and Alisha's reflections in the window. Diego bent his head over Alisha's and whispered something. Alisha bit her lip, then nodded slowly. They both broke into smiles. What were they sniggering about now?

"Issa, Diego specifically asked to have dinner with you tonight so you could meet Catalina."

She knew Catalina well enough, thanks.

"I have a feeling you two would make fine friends." Diego smiled at both girls. Issa inched even farther away from Cat. The girl could poison her right here in front of their parents without even batting her big fake eyelashes.

"Yeah, sure," Issa said instead. The sooner this pompous snob stopped talking, the better.

"Your mother says you have adjusted well at Athens."

Issa paused. Adjusted well. Right. She was the only student in the whole school whose parents weren't millionaires...and everyone knew it. The only ones who didn't care were Ishaan and Gigi. If it weren't for them, Issa would have spent the rest of her high-school years playing second tier to a bunch of spoiled East Coast princesses. Girls like Cat. Issa's cheeks started to burn again. It just wasn't fair. How could a horrible witch like Cat have everything? Money, friends, a fancy convertible...and now Adam. She hated Cat, hated her with every fiber of her soul.

"Why don't you come with me, Iz? We can fetch drinks for the parents," Catalina asked sweetly, turning to Issa, her velvet eyes widening.

Fetch drinks? What was this, a bad fifties movie?

"Dinner's almost ready, *mi hija*. Don't keep us waiting," Diego called behind them.

"Of course not, *Papi*."

Issa reluctantly followed Catalina, while glancing over her shoulder at her mother. Alisha and Diego were gazing at each other, Diego gently stroking her arm. Gross.

They had to get out of here. For good. Her mother could never see Diego again. Unfortunately, her mother looked happy and Diego was treating her like a queen. And Cat was acting like she'd gotten a personality transplant overnight.

Issa had her work cut out for her.

Catalina led Issa into a room that was less kitchen and more futuristic space station. She immediately started throwing open cabinets and pulled out a tiny shot glass and a bottle of Sprite. "I need good vodka to get through this dinner."

As soon as Cat took the top off the bottle, the strong smell of alcohol permeated the room.

Vodka in a Sprite bottle? Now, that was just ghetto.

Issa stood openmouthed and watched as Catalina poured herself a shot of the liquid, threw it into the back of her throat. "Actually I need two." Repeat.

"What the—" Issa should have known better than to trust Cat for even a moment.

"What, what're you going to do? Huh, *chica?* Tell Daddy on me?" Catalina sneered. "Please. I know how to handle him, okay? Don't get any ideas."

"Yeah, I bet."

"Yeah, whatever." Catalina carefully restashed her alcoholic paraphernalia and pulled a tin of Altoids from the same shelf. "I don't know what kind of game you and your brown-trash mom are playing."

Issa resisted the urge to slap Cat. "What the hell did you say? You think we want to be here? If your idiot of a father—"

"He's having some sort of midlife crisis obviously. Don't worry, your mother isn't that special."

Cat swallowed two Altoids and breathed into her hand. Apparently satisfied that the alcoholic scent was gone, she hid the box of mints. "He's decided he's going to be with her. I don't care. Up to him. But I'll tell you this." Cat stepped very close to Issa, all signs of innocence gone from her almond-shaped eyes. "One day when he realizes he's brought home mulatto trash, you'll be at the end of the driveway with the rest of the garbage."

Issa's brain raced. Diego was just playing Alisha. He had no idea about her background or ex-husband. When he found out this stupid love affair would be over so fast...

Cat brushed past Issa, shoving her shoulder into Issa's collarbone. "Get in the dining room. Smile. Act happy. Oh, and if you get in my way and think you can tattle on me to my dad, good luck. You think I made your life hell before? No, *chica,* that was nothing. You'll see exactly what I'm capable of."

Issa rubbed her bruised collar. The little tramp was pretty strong.

Cat swept into the dining room and Issa could practically hear her go through her Jekyll and Hyde transformation. "Issa's on her way," Cat announced sweetly.

Issa seethed. How could Alisha possibly think she and Cat would ever get along? The girl was evil, pure evil.

Dinner was torture. Diego had crafted a fine leg of lamb stewed in a tomato-and-onion curry served over white rice with a side of black beans. Any other day, Issa would have gobbled down such a gourmet meal. But today, it tasted like a *Fear Factor* delicacy in her mouth.

She avoided Cat's eyes while the girl jabbered on about

school and friends. Issa finally managed to swallow a few bites of food and pushed her plate away. It was almost over. As soon as they got home, Issa would explain everything to her mother. Surely, she would break up with Diego immediately and inform him of what a tramp his daughter was.

Issa peeked over at Cat's dish to see what anorexics ate nowadays. Surprisingly, Cat was chowing down on her leg of lamb and her plate was almost clean. Issa rolled her eyes. She wouldn't be surprised if Cat "excused herself" in about ten minutes to go to the bathroom and puke it all up.

"There's something…we'd like to discuss with you." The hesitation in Alisha's voice made Issa sit up straight from her half-slouchy pose. The "you tell her" expressions Alisha and Diego were exchanging did not look like good news.

"Issa, last weekend, I asked your mother to marry me."

CHAPTER 3

Everyone in Life Has a Purpose, Even If It's to Serve as a Bad Example

suddenly the room looked fuzzy and Alisha's voice was very far away. A delusion, a bad dream, a hallucination. This had to be anything but the truth. Issa was going to throw up.

"You're crazy, right?" Issa whispered, barely able to hear herself. There was a roaring in her ears, like the ocean, or gunfire. Then she realized it was the hammering of her heart.

"Issa, we're not...we're not joking." Alisha disentangled her hand from Diego's. "Diego is a good man, he cares about me a lot and this is going to be wonderful. You and Catalina will be sisters! I know we're going to love being a family."

Issa dared to glance over at Catalina to see how she was reacting. Knowing Cat's famous temper, Issa had a feeling this engagement was going to end here, tonight.

"Well, I think this..." Cat finally set her fork down and folded her hands. Issa took a deep breath. Here it came. Alisha would see what she was marrying into. "I think it's awesome! I mean, I've always wanted a big family. It's been Papi and me for so long."

To Issa's shock, she saw tears in Cat's eyes before she lowered them demurely.

What the hell was going on here? Cat *knew* about this. It had to be. That's what she'd been alluding to in the kitchen.

"You all crazy," Issa gasped after a moment's silence, nausea shooting up her throat. "All of you. Mom, you can't just marry this…" She shot her most ferocious look toward Diego, trying to contain her tears. "And his daughter! She's psycho! You guys have no idea and—"

"Issa!"

Issa realized she sounded insane, but didn't care. "She attacked me this morning. And then she warned me, and then Adam told me about her and the hot tub and now—You can't!"

Her head whirled from Cat to Diego to Alisha. Why was no one saying anything? Why was no one seeing her side?

"Issa, that's enough. Okay? Diego and I have made up our minds. I thought you would understand…." Alisha looked stricken.

"This is completely whack!" Issa threw down her napkin. "You can't marry him!" She gestured violently at Diego. "He doesn't know how to raise a kid, look at her!" She jabbed at Cat's direction. "She's the biggest bitch on earth!"

"Issa." Diego rose from the table. "This is not the time for a scene."

"You do *not* talk to me! You are *not* my daddy and you never will be," Issa snapped, and glared at Alisha.

"Issa." Alisha stood up quickly and grabbed Issa's arm.

"Please, everyone. Please excuse us. I need a minute alone with my daughter."

Alisha led Issa into the front hall. "What is the matter with you? I didn't raise you to be like—"

"Mom, no!" Issa whispered. "This ain't right! You don't know nothing about these people, and—"

Issa realized she'd completely lost her East Coast sheen. Right now she was the girl from the ghetto fighting for what she believed in.

"Stop it right now. You and I have always been the best of friends. I assume you would want my happiness. Yes?"

Issa was silent.

"Yes or no. You want my happiness?"

"Yes," Issa whispered, even though she had never felt further away from Alisha. "But don't you see what they think of us? They don't think we're good enough for them. Diego, he doesn't know about me, about Dad! And, Mom, she's crazy! She was throwing back shots in the kitchen and telling me—"

"Cat was nothing but sweet to you! I saw it with my own eyes. Issa, I know you don't like her, but please, you have to try."

Try? Try to like Cat Morena? That was like trying to like having her fingers chopped off one at a time. "You must be crazy! Cat's just—"

"Stop throwing this fit. Iz, this isn't like you. Diego and I are getting married over Christmas. Amir will be home. We'll all be together then, the whole family."

That selfish little bitch and her pushover father? They'd never be her family.

"That's not enough time," Issa protested. "I barely know these people. *You* barely know these people! How can you just marry someone you dated for a few months?"

"You have three months to get used to the idea. Diego has asked us to move into this house so we can all get used to living together. You and I are moving here next weekend."

CHAPTER 4

I'm an Angel, Honest! The Horns Are Just There to Keep the Halo Straight

"Amir, she has completely lost her mind," Issa shrieked into the phone as soon as her brother picked up.

"What now?" Amir, in his usual calm tone, didn't sound the slightest bit alarmed. His ability to remain unruffled by any drama was the key reason Amir was her anchor more than anyone. But right now, she really needed him to panic with her.

"She's actually going to make us move! She's packing!"

"Look, listen. You listening?"

"*Amir!*"

Silence on the phone and from the other bedroom where Alisha was packing. Issa felt like she was the only sane person in the world.

"Iz, why are you shrieking? I can hear you at a normal decibel too, you know. Quit being dumb."

"You're dumb," Issa muttered.

"Iz, stop it." Amir sighed. "I know what's going on here. It's not just Diego, is it?"

Issa scowled. No, it was also Cat. And Diego. And this whole stupid idea. Who got remarried when they had two grown-up children? She didn't need a stepfather. And she certainly didn't need Cat!

"Look, he's not coming back. Our daddy is not coming back. A man doesn't walk out the door one day, disappear and just come back five years later. You dig?"

In one second, Amir got to the heart of Issa's problem. The problem she didn't even know she was wrestling with until that moment.

Their father. Roy. After he left, it seemed everything had fallen apart. After the divorce papers arrived in the mail and Alisha was laid off from her job at the inner-city Detroit high school where she had taught art, Alisha, Amir and Issa had moved out of their brownstone. They had ended up in New Joliet for her mom's new job. The quaint, rich town where they were known as the "poor mixed family."

One day her father would come back, Issa knew he would. A man didn't just leave a note saying "Need to figure stuff out, will be back" and disappear forever. They would see him again. They would. They had to. But not if Alisha married Diego.

But Issa kept this fantasy her own secret. She knew Amir would never forgive their father for leaving them. "He's not a man," Amir always said. "A man would never do such a horrible thing. He was a coward."

Issa changed the subject back to Diego. "If it was anyone else it would be okay. But, Amir, you should see this man!

And Cat is horrible! You remember how she used to be, right? I hate their whole family, they're so spoiled and rotten and—"

"Shut up," Amir cut in. "This isn't you. You're acting insane."

Issa counted to five silently. Amir was right. She sounded insane. She had to pull herself together. She had to reasonably explain to Alisha why she could never, ever be related to *Cat Morena*.

Amir was still talking. "…get to know Cat. She doesn't have a mom, of course she's screwed up. And, Iz, you always get along with everyone. I know you'll win her over too."

No way. Not a chance. Not that manipulative, miserable—

"Look, after getting to know them, if you still don't like this situation, I'm sure Ma will listen to you."

Amir obviously had no idea what Cat was made of. A few nice sister-sister conversations wouldn't turn the Wicked Witch of the East Coast into an angel. Cat had decided long ago that Issa was an enemy. And that wasn't about to change. Cat would be around twenty-four-seven. The things she could do to Issa if they lived under the same roof…

"When are you coming home?" she asked instead.

"I can't for a while. Exams are going on, probably not till the wedding—"

"Amir…"

Issa's eyes started to fill as she thought of him being so far away. He had been the pillar of their family ever since their father had left them. How could he leave them and go so far away to attend college in Los Angeles? He'd only been gone for two months and already she missed him so much she called him every night.

"Give Mom a break. It hasn't been an easy few years for her. This new job, me going away. You growing up so fast…"

Issa sniffed. The years had been hard on her too. New school, new friends, her beloved father gone.

"Call once you guys are moved in, okay? And, Iz? Please try to behave!"

Yeah, right.

After Issa said her goodbyes, she reached into the drawer of her nightstand and pulled out a photograph. It was of her mother and father when they were young, just moving into Detroit where they'd lived a bohemian lifestyle for almost fifteen years. Roy and Alisha Bradley. Her father, as handsome as a young Ice Cube, was kissing Alisha's hand. Alisha had her head thrown back with laughter. Issa hadn't seen her mother laugh like that since her father had left.

"Come back, Daddy," Issa whispered. "Come back and let's get our old life back. Mom needs you so much right now. We need you."

She squeezed her eyes shut and tried to remember what her father sounded like. She could barely remember his scent. His voice no longer rang in her ears. They were forgetting him.

She heard the sound of her mother's singing in the next room as she packed her things. Issa had to stop this madness.

"Mom! We can't move into Diego's house! You can't live with him!" Issa threw herself on top of Alisha's bed, right in the center of a pile of clothes. "You guys aren't married. It's gross to live together. What will people say?" She knew she was really grasping here, but she had to make Alisha see reason.

"This love is making me roll. She said goodbye...too many times beforororor..." Alisha continued singing as she tossed her clothes haphazardly into boxes.

"Mom!"

"What?" Alisha finally stopped singing and flopped down onto her bed.

"You're messin' up the words." Issa took a deep breath and sat up straight. "Quit bein' all ghetto."

"Whatever."

"And would you please listen to me?" Issa snapped her fingers. "Why do we have to move to Diego's? Let's all get to know each other like we have been. He and Cat stay there. You and I stay here. The old-fashioned way. I think it's been going well, don't you?"

Actually it had been going horribly. Diego had insisted on cooking dinner at the Mazumder house on Thursday. Cat had strolled around the house and snickered at their second-hand furniture while Issa had hidden in her room. More than ever, Issa was sure this marriage was a match made in hell.

Alisha raised an eyebrow. "Could this have anything to do with your little issue with Cat?"

"Little issue?" Issa was disbelieving. "Do you not hear a word I'm saying'? Those people are crazy! We cannot live in their house!"

"Why do you hate them so much?"

"I don't...hate him, I don't even know him. But neither do you. You've dated him for like, what, two months? You can't just marry the first guy that asks."

"I know you're not going to understand this, but Diego is good for me. And he'll be good for you too. He's stable and has a great job—"

"Mama, please! This is why you ran away from your parents' house. They wanted you to marry some rich person like Diego."

It was true. If there was one thing Alisha hated, it was losing her freedom. She'd refused to give in to her parents' "marry a rich guy" pressure and had run away with starving-writer Roy instead.

Alisha rolled her eyes. "I ran away because I loved your father and wanted to be with him. And I wanted my own life outside of being a housewife."

"And because you didn't want to marry somebody just for the sake of convenience," Issa reminded her. She'd heard the story of her mother running away from home a zillion times. How could Alisha forget the suffocating life she'd left behind so quickly?

"And that, yes. But Diego isn't for convenience. Believe me, having you throw these fits is not even slightly convenient." Alisha wasn't even slightly ruffled as she tossed a mound of floor-length skirts, V-necked tops and long scarves into a suitcase.

Issa ignored the teasing tone. This was serious. How could Alisha throw away their fun, lighthearted lives for a cold mansion and a dysfunctional family? "Do you love him?"

"He cares a lot for me, and you too. And I care a lot about him."

"So you don't love him."

Alisha was silent.

I didn't think so.

Issa knew her mom would never love anyone the way she'd loved her father. All the Diegos in the world wouldn't matter to Alisha if Roy came back.

Issa was convinced more than ever that this wedding could not take place. No matter what it took or how much she broke Alisha's heart.

"The Morenas suck," Issa muttered instead of voicing her opinion about her father. Alisha would laugh at her and tell her to stop dreaming. "Especially Cat."

"Why are you so nasty to her? It makes *you* look bad. Not her," Alisha said. "She seems perfectly sane."

Issa's ears burned. Cat? Sane? Frightening thought. "You don't understand. Adam dumped me in front of the whole school...for her!"

Alisha stood on the bed and started to take down the Picasso *Violin and Guitar* print on the wall. "I have to agree with Cat. If Adam broke up with you, he's an idiot. That's not her fault, babe."

Issa rolled her eyes. Adam did have some help in his realization that she wasn't the girl for him. Like Cat's bikini-clad body wrapped around him in her daddy's hot tub.

The thought made Issa sick.

"Do you remember my freshman year when those three girls went to the headmaster and said I'd cheated on the biology final by looking at notes I'd hidden in my sleeve? The test I got a perfect score on? That was Cat and her friends."

Alisha looked down at Issa. "Why would you say that? Do you have proof?"

"I don't need proof! We were lab partners for like a

week and we were almost friends. Then she asked me to do her lab for her and I told her no way. She swore she would get me and she did. I could have gotten kicked out of school!"

"Why didn't you tell me it was Cat? You told me it was some random chick who hated you for no reason!"

Issa picked at the embroidery on the bedspread with her nail. "Everyone made fun of me for being the teacher's kid. I didn't want you doing anything else for me. I thought I would be able to handle Cat on my own."

She hated bringing Alisha into her petty school fights. Bad enough that she was "different" for being poor and a mixed-breed. She didn't need to be the girl who had to have her mommy save her all the time.

"Well, I respect you for handling things on your own. But, babe, that was such a long time ago. And things are different now. You guys are going to be sisters. She's going to be nicer to you."

"Uh, no!"

"Uh…yes! Listen, Cat's had a tough past…" Alisha's voice trailed off as she rolled her art print and fastened it tightly with a rubber band taken from her wrist.

"What do you mean? You mean, she didn't drive a sports car once upon a time?" Issa felt no sympathy for the poor little rich girl's unfortunate history.

"Cat's mom died when she was really young. She grew up with nannies because Diego was busy with his job, so she never learned to get along with people…and she never learned how to study."

No big shock there. Cat was infamous for her pathetically low grades. Everyone knew she stayed in school only because of Diego's generous contribution.

"When Cat took my class this year, I saw that she had talent. I asked Diego to come in to talk about his daughter's future. Diego told me he was so happy to hear that I believed in Cat, because every other teacher in her life tells him that she's never going to amount to anything."

Harsh. But still, Cat deserved it.

Alisha reached over and hugged Issa. "Diego has spoiled her to make up for a lack of family. She's lonely. She and Diego aren't friends like we are. He's a dad and she's a kid. That's how things work in their house. She needs us."

Issa didn't buy it.

"Their house isn't like ours. They're not a democracy," Alisha continued. "Diego makes the rules and expects Cat to obey. He told Cat months ago that he was seeing me and he told her last week we were getting married. And that Cat was getting a new stepsister with whom she'd be sharing all her lavish things."

Aha.

It explained everything. Why Cat had reignited her hatred for Issa after almost two years of leaving her alone. She was *warning* Issa about what her life would be like if this wedding took place. Cat couldn't break up the engagement, Diego would never allow it. *Issa* would have to be the bad guy here.

Issa groaned at the revelation. She had to do the un-doable. All alone.

"Come on, babe." Alisha was still holding Issa. "I need you to give them a chance, okay?"

Issa could feel herself weakening. Alisha was her best

friend and she had sacrificed so much for her and Amir. She could try to deal with Cat. For her mother's sake at least.

But not without one last-ditch effort to bail.

"Mama—come on—" Issa whined. "You're really going to ruin your precious baby girl's life? Your last born? The light of your life?"

"Buy you that leather-bound version of *Pride and Prejudice* you have your eye on if you pack without any more whining." Alisha had an amused glint in her eye.

"Are you bribing me?" Issa asked. "You expect me to fall for this—this—"

"Why, yes, I do."

"Mom!" Issa grinned despite herself. How did Alisha do it? Alisha had a way about her, she could enchant anyone within the hour.

And Diego was no exception. Issa sighed. It was up to her to undo what Alisha had done. If her mother wasn't willing to listen, maybe Diego would.

As Issa sadly lined her jasmine and gardenia candles into a box and folded her sari curtains on top, she formulated a plan. If she knew one thing about Diego, it was that he was all about appearances. Issa knew she could play on that.

As she finished removing every glowy star from the ceiling, she glanced around the barren room. She would miss this place. If everything went well, she and Alisha would be moving back in no time.

After the bulging moving trucks pulled away from the driveway at precisely 5:45 p.m., Issa pounced on Alisha. "Let's get going. I want to make sure I get a bigger bathroom than you." Issa turned her eyes so her mother couldn't see into them. She'd never been able to lie to Alisha and she wouldn't put it past her mother to call her out on her little plan now.

Alisha tousled Issa's bangs absently. "Thanks, babe. I knew you'd come around."

Score. Alisha seemed too distracted to notice her daughter's newfound eagerness to get to Casa Morena.

Issa felt only slightly guilty as she practiced her speech to Diego in her head on the car ride over. As the car puffed up to the driveway, Issa tried to sound casual.

"Hey, Mom, could you give me just a few minutes with Diego? I want to apologize for being such a pain."

Alisha looked pleasantly surprised. "Sure, hon. I'll wait here."

"Thanks."

Confronting Diego had seemed like a good idea when she was safe in their little town house, but standing here in front of Casa Morena, Issa felt completely out of place and ter-rified. Or as Gigi would say, like wrong-side-of-the-tracks Ryan Atwood during his first day in the O.C.

God, she wished Gigi or Ishaan were by her side right now. She hated knowing she was all alone in her battle.

"Hello, and welcome, Issa." Diego opened the door with a flourish after Issa forced her thumb to ring the bell. "Cat-alina is out with friends, but she will be back for dinner."

Goody.

Issa stepped inside, lugging the huge garbage bag filled with her stuffed animals behind her. The entry looked even more gigantic than she remembered. How was she going to live here? The marble staircase leading upstairs seemed to go on and on. This place needed an elevator.

"Mom's tipping the movers and I wanted to talk to you alone for a sec." Issa shifted the bag to her other hand and stared at the pristine white floor.

Diego closed the front door with a puzzled look on his face. "Of course."

"Listen, Mr. Diego, Mr. Morena, Mr. Diego, sir…"

"You may call me Diego, if I may call you Issa," Diego said with a hint of a smile.

Issa almost smiled too. Diego had just made a joke. And it was almost funny for an old guy. Weird. "Okay, Diego. Um, I think it looks kind of wrong for me and Mom to live here, you know. I mean, we're Indian. I mean, you know that, what I mean is…"

Issa could feel redness rising in her cheeks. This was not going as predicted. The speech had sounded so good in the car, but now she just sounded confused.

"What I mean is that you guys are going to be living together. And she teaches at the school and she's a role model person, right? I don't want my mom getting a reputation as living with guys before she's married." The words tumbled out of her mouth before she could figure out a way to make them sound pretty.

Diego was silent for a minute. "I completely understand. It's not very common for us either. To cohabit before marriage, I mean."

Issa shifted from foot to foot.

"Cubans are quite traditional, you know. So, this 'living together' as they call it, would be frowned on in my family."

Issa didn't know what to say. "Um, yeah. Cohabiting. Bad." Was she really going to get through to him? Could this horrible move actually be called off?

"What I actually had in mind was that, you and your mother would move into our guest house," Diego said, reaching out and taking the heavy bag from Issa's hand.

They had a guest house? Like in *The O.C.*? Gigi was going to flip.

"Uh, what?"

Diego pointed to the side of the house. "Next to the pool is a very cozy cottage. Bedrooms, full kitchen. I think you both will be very comfortable there. The four of us can share all our meals together here and you two can retreat there for the nights. How is that? Until the wedding, of course."

Issa stuttered. "That sounds, um—" *not* what she had in mind, but at least she wouldn't be under the same roof as Cat Morena "—very nice. Thanks, Diego."

"You're most welcome. And, Issa," he called as she started for the front door. "I'd like a moment alone with your mother."

Yuck!

"Why don't you go through the kitchen door and explore your new place? I think you'll like the indoor pool."

Pool? Wow. Issa grinned openly this time. "Thanks again."

Maybe he wasn't such a bad guy after all. Too bad his daughter was a psychopath.

"I can't believe you live here now!" Gigi bounced up and down on Issa's bed. "This is only the guest house? This is bigger than the houses on *The Real World!*"

Issa had to agree. The Morena guest house was pretty much a miniature version of the mansion with its own sunroom, four bedrooms, a hot tub and an indoor pool. As soon as she'd seen it, she'd called Ishaan and Gigi from her cell phone and demanded they come over so she could show off her new place.

"I feel like we could play soccer in here." Ishaan was equally in awe of Issa's new bedroom. Complete with vaulted sixteen-foot ceilings and a walk-in closet the size of Issa's old bedroom, the room was at least a thousand square feet and the king-sized bed took up only one tiny corner of it. "What are you going to do with all this space?"

"She needs to shop and fill it!" Gigi tossed her tumbling red curls over her shoulder, her green eyes dancing with excitement. "You need to grab Diego's credit card, Iz. Let's go next weekend!"

The thought had crossed her mind. What did they do about money now? Diego seemed to have so much of it, and as far as she could see, he was pretty generous about doling it out. But still, he wasn't her daddy and if luck had anything to do with it, he and Alisha would realize getting married was a stupid idea and this whole arrangement could be over soon.

"He's not my dad. I'd feel weird spending his money."

Unless he insisted, of course.

Issa finally hung up the last of her clothes and joined Gigi on the bed. Her pathetic wardrobe barely made a dent in the vast closet and she couldn't imagine her threadbare sari curtains or plastic glowy stars in here.

"You could make this into a dance studio." Gigi stood

on the edge of the bed again, her arms out at her sides. Issa scooted to the very edge of the bed to keep from getting fallen on.

"Or a game room." Ishaan started shoving Issa's stack of novels into a bookshelf. "You could do like a pool table and some video games—"

"Or that *Arabian Nights*–like lounge we're always talking about!" Gigi squealed and threw herself backward into the bed again. "Oh, heaven. I could get used to this."

Issa giggled. At least one of them was having a good time. She heard the sound of the front door open and close, then the click of Alisha's heels.

"Ahh…the prodigal friends return." Her mother leaned in the doorway of Issa's bedroom, a smile on her face. "Haven't seen you crazy kids in a while."

Finally back from her talk with Diego, Alisha was glowing. Issa watched her try to hide a smile and wondered what it meant.

"Alisha!" Gigi shrieked. "Congratulations!" She was off the bed and throwing herself into Alisha's arms before Issa could blink.

"Thanks, honey."

"God, Alisha. Look at that rock!"

"I know!" Alisha flashed her left hand in the air. An unfamiliar diamond sparkled on her ring finger.

So that was it. It was officially official. Alisha and Diego were formally engaged. Issa blinked away a sudden rush of tears in her eyes. Her mom had given up all hope of her father coming back.

Issa wished she could be as happy as Gigi was for her mother. She wished she could just enjoy this new luxury and not worry about the future. Unfortunately, with Cat Morena living a hundred yards away, Issa couldn't help but feel an overwhelming sense of doom.

Issa turned so Alisha wouldn't see the dejected look on her face. Instead, Ishaan saw her face and shot her a sympathetic look. He understood how much she missed her father and what this engagement meant.

Issa smiled at him. As much as she loved Gigi, her friend could be a bit of a flake. Issa knew she could always count on Ishaan to know how she really felt.

Gigi dragged Alisha over to the bed, peppering her with questions. "So, when are you guys getting married? Is Issa going to be in the wedding? Where's it going to be?"

"The wedding will be sometime in mid-December. And as for where, we have no idea. And if Issa wants to be in it, she is more than welcome." Alisha smiled and touched Issa's hand. "It'll be wonderful to have both Cat and Issa in the wedding."

Issa shuddered. Yeah, sure. And Cat would become a nun the week after too.

"*Hola?* Anyone home?"

Speak of the devil.

Cat poked her head into Issa's bedroom. "*Papi* has asked that you both come to the main house for dinner."

"Hey, Cat." Alisha smiled at the arrival. "You know Issa's friends, Gigi and Ishaan, right? Come on in."

Issa grimaced as Cat strolled in and took a seat next to Alisha. Even though Cat's Sunshine and Jewel were on the same cheerleading team as Gigi, Gigi had no tolerance for mean people and refused to hang out with their clique. That made Gigi enemy material in Cat's book.

"Yeah, of course! Hey, Geeg!"

Geeg?

Gigi looked pretty confused herself. "Uh, hey, Cat."

"So, Ishaan." Cat arched her feet, showing off her long legs. "That was a really amazing goal you made last weekend. I think you're the hottest star on our soccer team."

Was she actually flirting with Ishaan? She'd never glanced at him twice before. Was it a subconscious thing she did, flirt with any male creature in a ten-foot vicinity? Now, *that* was ghetto.

"Oh…thanks." Ishaan finished placing the last of the books in the shelves and ran a hand nervously through his wavy hair. "But I'm not really."

"They should make you the captain. I watch all your games, you know," Cat practically purred, her eyelashes batting. "What do you think, Issa?"

God, what was her problem? Issa opened her mouth to voice exactly what she thought, but Ishaan cut in. "Um, thanks," he muttered, and grabbed Gigi's arm. "We should go now. Gigi has to, uh, wash her hair."

"Hey!" Gigi's protest was cut off by Ishaan dragging her to the door.

Issa stood and escorted her friends. "See what I mean?" she murmured.

"Totally. Hitting on Ishaan like that. What a fake!" Gigi said indignantly, pulling her faux-fur coat over her shoulders. Issa almost laughed. Her secret crush on Ishaan didn't seem so secret when she got so upset when another girl flirted with him.

Ishaan hung back for a second as Gigi stomped out of the guest house. He placed a hand on the small of Issa's back, whispering in her ear, "Watch out for Cat. She seems like she's up to something."

Gigi watched them curiously from the doorway. "Coming, Ishaan?"

"Yeah, coming." Ishaan squeezed Issa's hand one last time and grabbed his jacket. "Bye, Iz."

Issa watched them get into Ishaan's Jeep. She wished more than anything that she was going with them.

Instead, she felt a rush of perfumed air as Cat and Alisha brushed past her, Alisha grabbing her hand. "Come, come."

At the house, Diego had created another masterpiece. Pork chops cooked with *mojito,* a mix of garlic, sour orange juice and olive oil. Issa was already completely in love with the side dishes of *tostanes,* friend plantains and yuca, a vegetable she'd never eaten before, along with the standard white rice and black beans. She hated her living situation but loved this food.

As Issa practically licked her plate clean, she had to admit there were some perks to living with the Morenas. Despite being an important lawyer Diego insisted on cooking a full three-course dinner every night for his family. And the desserts she'd spotted in the kitchen had her mouth watering already.

"So, now that you girls are all settled in the guest house, let's discuss the house rules," Diego announced as he returned to the table with four tiny cups of *café con leche,* crazy strong coffee served with hot whole milk.

House rules? What was this, boarding school? Issa shot

Alisha a look. The only house rules they'd had was no staying out all night without calling, no jumping from the roof without a parachute and no watching *Sex and the City* episodes unless they were both present.

"Rule number one. We have dinner every night together. 7:00 p.m. sharp. This is the time we talk about our days."

Issa relaxed. Not too bad. So she would be forced to eat these four-star meals every day. The worst that would happen was she would put on an extra ten pounds. She could deal.

"Rule number two. If either of you girls wants to see a young man socially, Alisha and I have to meet him first and approve him."

Young man? Issa fought back the urge to giggle. Alisha's way of approving Issa's *young men* was to flirt with them till they became uncomfortable.

She had a feeling Diego's approval was going to be a lot tougher.

"Rule number three. No interrupting me when I am working in my den or when I'm watching baseball games."

"Which is, like, all the time," Cat muttered.

Issa rolled her eyes. Poor little rich girl couldn't stand to have Daddy's attention on anything but her.

"Rule number four. We are a family and will act as such. We will share everything. There is no mine and hers business."

Issa stopped smiling. Exactly what he expected her to share with Cat was beyond her. Her homework? Cat would love that.

"Now, let's figure out transportation." Diego set his fork down. "Issa needs a car."

Cat scowled.

"Diego, no," Alisha interrupted. "Issa has walked to school all these years and I give her a ride when the weather turns bad. This isn't necessary."

Issa looked up from her water glass. She begged to differ. She'd never had her own car and wasn't about to look Diego's gift horse in the mouth. Unfortunately, a stern look from her mother shut her up from voicing her opinion.

"Um, yeah. I don't need a car. Mom can take me. Really. It's not that far of a walk from here. Just like five miles or something." Issa tried to sound as pathetic as possible.

It worked.

Diego looked from Alisha to Issa. "Absolutely no walking. Issa will get her own car, but for now, Cat, I want you to give a spare key to the Lotus to Issa."

"*Papi!*"

"Cat—"

"No, *Papi!* It's mine! You gave it to me for my birthday!"

"Catalina Santiago Morena! Rule number four! Issa will soon be your sister. I expect you both to act that way. Is that understood?"

No one moved. Alisha poked Issa in the side.

"Yes, Diego," Issa muttered.

"Catalina?" Diego turned his fiery eyes on Cat. "*Comprende?*"

"*Sí, Papi.*" Cat's voice quavered as her eyes filled with tears.

It seemed that Cat's privileged life was crumbling around her. Issa felt a sense of smugness as Cat pushed her chair back from the table.

"I'm going upstairs," Cat mumbled before running out of the room.

The table fell silent. Issa felt Alisha's eyes on her. She knew her mother expected her to fix the problem to keep the peace in their new family.

"I'll go to talk to her." Issa stood up with a sigh, even though she planned to do no such thing. Let Cat stay upset for a night. Finally, she got to experience a fraction of what Issa was feeling.

As Issa left the dining room, she heard Cat's stiletto heels thump up the stairs. How the mighty had fallen.

Finally. Cat Morena would finally know what it was like to have something she loved be taken away. Issa paused in the driveway to run her finger over the hood of the hot-pink Lotus convertible. She would love to ride in this someday.

Maybe this living with the Morenas wouldn't be so bad after all.

CHAPTER 5

If Everything Seems to be Going Well, You've Obviously Overlooked Something

"**Hey**, Diego." Issa slid into a chair across from him in the breakfast nook the next morning and checked out the time. She was supposed to meet Professor Kidlinger in twenty minutes about her independent-study project.

"Good morning."

"Do you know where my mom is?"

Diego glanced at her over the *Daily News*. "She had to go early for a staff meeting. Is there something I can help you with?"

"Oh, um." Issa's cheeks burned. "I was going to ask her to give me a ride. Usually I would just call a friend, but I need to get to school to meet my English prof and—"

Diego immediately set his paper down. "Why, Issa, you will go with Cat. That car is for your use, as well, now."

Already? Cat was going to kill her. Maybe that wasn't

such a good idea so early in the game. Maybe she could call Ishaan and get a ride.

"Uh, it's okay." Issa cleared her throat, realizing talking to Diego made her voice abnormally whispery. "I'll just call a friend. Thanks, though."

"Nonsense." Diego stood up and got another glass from the cabinet, which he filled with fresh orange juice. He slid the glass across the table to Issa. "You will drive together from now on. Cat and you will soon be sisters. Sisters share everything. It's time Cat learned that."

"Cat learned what?" Cat paused as she entered the kitchen, glancing suspiciously at Issa.

"To share, *mi hija*." Diego held out an arm for his daughter. "You'll ride with Issa in the Lotus today. If she'd like to drive, please be courteous and allow her to do so."

"Just a ride to school will be fine," Issa interrupted, trying to control the damage that was sure to come. "Thanks, Cat."

Issa could swear Cat's head was about to start spinning, *Exorcist*-style. "What!"

"I'm ready whenever you are." Issa hid her face behind the glass of juice.

"*Papi!*"

"Catalina Santiago Morena! Rule number—"

"Yeah, yeah, ix-nay on the boys, baseball interruption, and not sharing. I get it. Whatever," was all Issa heard Cat mutter as she stomped into the garage.

The ride to school was silent and uneventful, except for the occasional death stare Cat shot Issa. As worried as Issa had been about Cat pulling a *Vanilla Sky* and driving them off a bridge, she couldn't help but feel a tad bit pleased. Diego was really enforcing his house rules. Maybe Cat would learn this transition wasn't going to be as smooth as she'd expected.

Issa—one. Cat—zero.

Issa had to admit, she understood how Cat could be on a power trip all the time. As the two girls pulled up at Athens Academy in the cotton-candy-colored Lotus Elise, heads turned. The crowd parted in front of Cat's parking spot as she eased the tiny car into the spot. Issa noticed the envious stares as Cat revved the engine one last time and turned off the ignition. Issa felt like a movie star.

"Don't expect this again. Find your own rides from now on," Cat snapped as she snatched up her Louis Vuitton bag.

Issa eyed it. A real Louis Vuitton. Not a cheap NYC Chinatown knockoff like the one Issa had hidden in her closet. Not fair. Why were some people just born lucky?

"You're the one that said you don't care if your dad gets married. Get used to sharing," Issa snapped back.

Not believing she actually dared to say that out loud, Issa flipped her hair behind her shoulder as she carefully closed the passenger-side door. She did her best "Cat walk," one foot in front of the other, head held high, as she marched into school.

"What was that!" Issa heard Gigi's distinct screech a second before her friend grabbed her arm. "You get Cat's car now too? Holy mama, this is a pretty sweet deal!"

"I know!" Issa whispered. "Diego yelled at Cat last night and told her she had to give me a ride whenever I want."

"Suddenly being a princess doesn't suck so bad, does it?" Gigi could barely hide the envious tone in her voice.

Issa realized she was smiling smugly, but she couldn't help it. Her smugness lasted exactly thirty more seconds till she crossed the hallway to her locker.

Adam was pressed against Issa's locker. Rather, he was *being* pressed onto her locker. By Cat. They were kissing, Adam's face contorted in pure bliss as Cat ran her fingers through his hair and ground her pelvis into his.

Issa froze.

"You want me to kick his ass now?" a low voice came from behind her. Ishaan was jamming his foot against the watercooler and glowering, not taking his eyes off Adam and Cat for an instant. "She ran in five seconds ago, grabbed Adam away from his idiot friends and practically threw him up against your locker." Ishaan shifted his toasted hazelnut-colored eyes to Issa. "She's playing with you."

"I'm gonna be sick," Issa whispered, spinning around to face anywhere else.

Gigi looked like she was going to cry. "I hate him! How can he do this to you?"

"That's it. Hold this." Ishaan shoved his physics book into Gigi's hands.

Issa held her breath. This was about to get ugly. As horrified as she was by the spectacle, a tiny twinge inside her was pleased Ishaan cared enough about her to be so angry. She had a feeling she was witnessing chivalry in the making.

"What's he doing?" Issa was too afraid to turn around.

"He's going up to them. Oh my God, he just grabbed Adam by the neck. Cat just jumped away. God, you have to see this!"

"Stop it!" Cat shrieked.

Issa dared to turn around.

Ishaan had Adam by the collar, Adam's freckled neck shading into a fierce red.

"You were never good enough for Iz. You know that, and I know that. Take the slut and get the hell out of here. Now!" Ishaan released Adam's collar and Adam's head hit the locker with a slam. "If I see you again, I swear to God…"

Issa bit her lip. She hadn't wanted Adam to get hurt. She thought Ishaan would just threaten him. This fight didn't seem fair. Ishaan was a star athlete and Adam could barely climb a flight of stairs without reaching for his asthma inhaler.

She stepped forward and was about to tell Ishaan to back off. Before she could, Adam met Ishaan's eyes defiantly and took Cat's hand. "Let's go, baby."

Issa could feel the tears start to well up. *I won't cry. Not here. Not now.*

"*Someone's* not handling this breakup well, are they?" Cat straightened her tiered miniskirt and swung her purse over her shoulder, arrogant smile returning to her face.

No, she wasn't handling the breakup well. And Adam knew her better than almost anyone. How could he treat her this way? Shoving this stupid new relationship in her face?

"Let's go somewhere else, Cat," Adam murmured, not looking at Issa.

"Oh, don't worry, Adam." Cat threaded her arm through his. "Issa's just feeling a bit insecure. Being a charity case and all. I mean, my dad has her and her mommy in the guest house living like queens. For now anyway.

As soon as he gets sick of the trash he's picked up, they'll be back out on the street."

Issa gritted her teeth and noticed a crowd had formed to see what all the commotion was about. A group of perfectly layered haired, label-conscious girls who called themselves the Belles were watching Issa with hawk eyes. They'd never even glanced at her before. Issa treated them the way she thought of all the "popular" girls, avoidance with a slight dash of fear.

Right now Issa had something in common with the Belles. All of them hated Cat. Issa turned her attention back to the locker drama at hand.

Ishaan took a murderous step toward Adam after Cat's latest comment. Adam quickly grabbed Cat's arm. "Come on, babe. Let's go."

"Um, yeah, I don't think so. This little bitch can kiss my—" Adam dragged Cat away before she could finish her sentence.

The Belles glanced at each other and then back at Issa. Pity showed on their faces before they walked away, their stilettos clicking and miniskirts swaying in sync.

Issa sniffed back her tears. She was so pathetic. Everyone at school was feeling sorry for her. This wasn't the time to lose it. Ishaan had been right about one thing. Adam wasn't good enough for her. He had never loved her. If he had, he would never have treated her this way. She unclenched her hands, realizing she'd left deep indents in her palms from her unclipped nails.

"Sorry about that," Ishaan murmured as he took his books back from Gigi. "I lost it. I can't stand it when—"

Without finishing the sentence, he shook his head and took off down the hallway, Gigi staring adoringly after him.

"God, he's amazing."

"Amazing?" Issa stared at his retreating back. It was pretty amazing the way he'd come to her rescue. He was like another big brother to her. So protective. But today, it almost seemed like he was personally vesting himself in the situation.

Issa didn't know whether to be flattered or concerned at how personally he was taking this whole Adam business.

"Do you think he would go out with me?" Gigi asked as Issa opened her locker. "I mean, like dating, not friends."

Issa considered this. Ishaan had never dated anyone. Sure, he'd taken girls who were friends to Homecoming but never had a real girlfriend. He was a good-looking guy, but she still didn't understand what *Gigi* saw in him. He wasn't the usual dumb-jock type Gigi liked. Ishaan was a lone wolf. He was good at school and good at sports, but didn't belong to any cliques. Issa knew he had a mysterious side and she didn't know if Gigi would be able to handle that.

"It's up to you, girl. Sure he's your type?" Issa avoided looking at Gigi. The truth was, the thought of her two best friends together made her feel weird. The only thing they seemed to have in common was their friendship with her. On top of every other change going on in her life, Issa was afraid the dynamics of their friendship would change if Ishaan and Gigi started to date. They would have their own thing going and she would be the third wheel.

"He's hot. And when he gets that look in his eye, like he knows what he wants and he's going to get it. Ooh, he's so sexy then." Gigi's eyes went soft and dreamy.

Issa smiled. Gigi's idea of sexy ranged from Usher to Seth Cohen on *The O.C.* to Ishaan Banerjee. Her friend was just plain boy-crazy. Despite this, Issa had to admit Ishaan *was* intensely sexy, much more so than the average seventeen-year-old guy.

"Then, yeah, ask him, I guess." Issa shut her locker, wanting to change the topic. Knowing Gigi, she would lose interest in this mission by the end of second period.

"Iz?" Gigi didn't move. "I need a favor."

Issa knew what was coming and she didn't like the idea one bit. "Uh-uh. I don't think so."

"Please! Please, please, please! You know him so much better than I do. You guys have that Indian family connection thing. Just find out if he's interested. But don't tell him I like him!"

"Gig—" This was a conversation she never thought she would have to have with Ishaan. What would she say, how would she start? What if he said yes? Her skin prickled at the thought. Right now, she was one of the most important people in Ishaan's life. That would change if he started dating Gigi. She would be left all alone. First ditched by Alisha for Diego, then ditched by Ishaan for Gigi.

"Please, Iz! I'll love you forever!"

"You already do." Issa smiled grudgingly. She was being unfair. Gigi was her friend. Gigi would certainly do the same for her.

"Please?"

Issa sighed. "If it comes up, I'll ask him."

The chances of that particular topic ever coming up was slim, and Issa managed to put the mission out of her head.

Unfortunately, she had just the right window of opportunity that afternoon after English class.

Ishaan refused to let her ride home with Cat and offered her a ride home in his Jeep. The walk to his car was silent with Issa wondering if she really had to bring the dreaded topic up.

Now or never.

"Yo, Ishaan. Listen." Issa hesitated as the car roared to life. She really didn't want to do this. She didn't want him to say he wanted to date Gigi. She didn't want anything else to change.

"'Sup?" He wove the car through the lanes of after-school traffic.

"You date girls, right?"

He took his eyes off the car in front of him. "You asking if I'm gay?"

"No! I mean…" She realized how idiotic that sounded. "I mean, you're willing to go out on dates, right? With girls."

"You asking me out?" Ishaan resumed staring straight ahead, smile on his lips.

"No!"

Mortifying. He'd saved her from her hideous ex-boyfriend and now it sounded like she was hitting on him. And did he have to look so amused at the thought?

Hmph. "I mean. Not for me. For Gigi. I figured. You're single. She's single—"

"Gigi wants to date me?"

"No!" Issa practically choked. This was not going well. Why did she agree to this? "I figured, you're both my friends. You're both nice people. Why shouldn't you guys date?"

Ishaan said nothing as if waiting for her to go on.

"So, what do you think?" Issa prodded. He was not making this easy. Gigi owed her big-time.

"Uh. Okay."

"Okay, you want to date her, or okay you're both nice? Ishaan, quit bein' all ghetto and give me a real answer." Issa was growing more and more exasperated. She could feel her bangs start to frizz from the nervous perspiration on her forehead. Ishaan was one of the most straightforward guys she knew. He hated games. She couldn't understand why he wasn't giving her a straight answer here. Either he wanted to date Gigi or not.

Ishaan slowed down the car as they entered the neighborhood of the Morena mansion. "Listen, Gigi's a nice girl. And she's cute, but I'm not looking for a casual fling right now."

Fling? Gigi was going to be *pissed* if she ever found out she was considered to be fling material rather than take-home-to-Mom material. Hopefully Ishaan would keep that tidbit of info to himself. But even Issa had to agree that she had a hard time imagining fun-loving Gigi dealing with day-to-day fights and a long-term commitment. Especially with someone as intense and loyal as Ishaan.

"You could get serious about Gigi," Issa protested half-heartedly. "She acts like a ditz, but she's really sweet and—"

"Iz."

"But she is!"

"Iz."

"What?"

"There's someone else."

"Oh."

That shut Issa up. Not what she'd been expecting. Ishaan had never shown any interest in a particular girl. Sure, he'd discreetly check out any pretty girl who would walk by, but never a second glance. Now there seemed to be someone real on the horizon. Issa didn't understand why he'd never mentioned her. Especially to her, one of his best friends. She never kept anything from him. He knew her every pathetic, silly secret. So why not the other way around?

After a second, she dared to look at Ishaan again, slightly stung that he was so casually keeping things from her. "Who is it?"

"Just someone." Ishaan sighed. "She's not available to me right now, though. But maybe one day. Till then, I don't want to waste anyone else's time, you know?"

"Yeah. I know."

Actually Issa didn't know. And that was really bothering her. How could she not know? Had she been so cocooned in her own little Cat Morena–Adam Mitchell world that she was now oblivious to her friends' problems?

"Look who's home." Ishaan parked the Jeep in front of the mansion next to the Lotus. "She must have ducked out to avoid you."

"Yeah." Issa's mind was somewhere else. She thought she knew Ishaan, but she'd never had even an inkling about this secret crush. This didn't speak much for their friendship. Issa noticed Ishaan's eyes passing over the Lotus again.

Hmm.

What if Ishaan was lying about it being "just someone"? What if it was Cat? His having it bad for Cat would definitely explain him not telling her and making it a point to keep his crush a secret.

It would also explain him breaking up the scene with Cat and Adam with the ferociousness he'd demonstrated that morning. Jealousy.

She glanced over at Ishaan. Was he one of the legions of guys at the high school who were dying to get into Cat's hot tub?

"You okay?" Ishaan broke into her thoughts. "What's up?"

"Nothing. I need go in and deal with Her Highness." Issa watched him carefully. Was that a wince in his eyes?

"Good luck."

"Uh, thanks for the ride."

"No prob. And, Iz? Tell Gigi I would love to go out with her, but I was afraid she'd break my heart, okay?"

Iz smiled. Ishaan could see right through her pathetic covering for Gigi. She wished she had the same gift and was able to see through him. "Sure, I'll tell Gigi. She's going to be disappointed, though."

She closed the door of the Jeep and glanced at Cat's bedroom window in the Morena mansion. Was Cat Ishaan's secret lady love?

CHAPTER 6

When Someone Steals Your Man, There Is No Better Revenge Than Letting Her Keep Him

"Oh, hello, Issa." Diego was sauntering down the swirling staircase as Issa swung open the front door.

"Have you seen my mom?" Issa blurted out. She still didn't know what to say to Diego. He made her nervous, as if she should curtsy in his presence or something.

"Alisha is in my study. I recently acquired some sketches by one of her favorite artists. Matisse. Some of his early works, it seems."

Lured in Mom with Matisse.

Issa wondered what it cost him to get those sketches. No way would original Matisse sketches be cheap. Or for sale in the open. He had to be dabbling in black-market art prints.

"Also, I have some rare books you might be interested in. I have one of the first-edition copies of *Pride and Prejudice* among others. Your mother says that's your favorite book."

A first-edition Austen! Issa's breath caught. She didn't

give a damn where or how Diego had managed to get his hands on one. She had to have a look.

"It's my absolute favorite!" Issa blurted out. More and more, she was realizing that maybe this little setup at the Morena house wasn't too bad. A first-edition Austen? She could only dream of such things.

"I am most happy I picked it up, then. Also, Cat arrived home a while ago," Diego continued, his eyebrows knitting together. "She said she tried to look for you after school, but wasn't able to find you. Is this true?"

Issa gritted her teeth. It would be easy to snitch on Cat, but she would save her complaints to Diego about much more serious issues. Right now she was too excited about *Pride and Prejudice*.

"Oh, that's okay. I asked a friend for a ride and—"

"There you are, Iz!" Cat suddenly appeared from the living room. "I looked for you! But you were absolutely nowhere to be found. With your new boyfriend again? Naughty, naughty!" A sly smile crossed her face.

"Boyfriend?" Diego's eyebrows immediately separated and rose straight up. "I wasn't aware you were seeing someone. We have yet to meet this young man. Rule number two, Issa."

"What? I'm not seeing anyone!" Issa eyed Cat. What was she up to?

"Oh, really? Then *who* was that dashing guy who was so possessive of you this morning?" Cat continued, a huge smile on her face.

"Ishaan's just a friend." Issa's cheeks burned. She was sure Cat wouldn't want her to mention *what* Ishaan was saving her from. What game was Cat playing?

Cat giggled. "Daddy, don't you think it'll be so fun if Issa and her boyfriend double-dated with me and *my* boyfriend this weekend? The two almost-sisters, out together!"

Issa could feel all the heat leaving her face and her hands turning clammy. Suddenly she was freezing despite her sweatshirt.

Cat's boyfriend? She'd already brought Adam home and gotten him Diego-fied? So it was officially official. Cat Morena and Adam Mitchell. The year's junior class power couple.

"That's very thoughtful of you, Catalina. I think it's an excellent idea. But first we would have to meet Issa's new boyfriend, right, Issa?"

"But I don't have a—"

"Adam is here now, we're studying. Why don't you join us, Iz?" When Cat used her nickname it sounded malicious and exaggerated.

"I don't have my books and I need to find Mom, so, uh, maybe later." She prepared to turn on her heel and run far away.

"Why don't you join them, Issa?" Diego placed a hand on her shoulder. "Maybe you can help my Catalina understand algebra finally? Her friend is helping her also."

Issa swallowed. So this was what Cat was up to. She couldn't let Cat see that the thought of her and Adam, *together,* was shredding up her insides. She nervously wiped her hands on her worn-out sweats and grimaced realizing how grubby she looked. Cat was in a micromini skirt and a baby-doll T-shirt, looking adorable. Issa standing next to Cat would just reaffirm to Adam why he broke up with Issa in the first place.

Diego was staring at Issa curiously. Calling out Cat would only make Issa look petty. Especially now that Cat had convinced Diego that Issa already had a "naughty" new boyfriend.

"Okay. Why not?" she managed to choke out.

"Come, come!" Cat grabbed Issa's hand and dragged her into the living room, Diego looking on and smiling.

Kill me now, kill me now. Issa squeezed her eyes shut and opened them again. She was standing in the doorway of the living room. Adam was sitting on one of the white leather couches, algebra book open on his lap, his mouth open even wider.

"Look who's here!" Cat said enthusiastically. She plopped down on Adam's lap, tossed the algebra book onto the floor and nibbled Adam's ear. "Iz wants to study with us. Isn't that cute?" She ran a hand down Adam's neck to the top button of his shirt.

"Uh, yeah." Adam's freckles started to pop up like they always did when he was nervous. He attempted to shift slightly away from Cat and eyed Issa. He was no doubt remembering the scene from that morning.

Don't worry, Adam. Ishaan's not here to save me now.

"Don't be embarrassed, baby. We're all friends here," Cat purred. "You're so sexy. I don't know why I didn't see it before."

Issa made a choking sound in her throat and managed to blurt out with a quiver, "Actually I need to find my mom." Before she turned her back to hide the tears in her eyes, she caught a glimpse of Cat kissing down Adam's neck. "Let's go up to my room," Cat murmured.

I'm going to be sick.

As Issa dashed down the hallway to Diego's study, she was haunted by the sound of Cat's giggling as she heard two sets of footsteps hurry up the stairs.

How had Adam moved on so fast? She couldn't go for more than a few hours without thinking about him. She kept having imaginary conversations with him, telling him in her head all the silly little things that happened to her that day. She saw his face in her dreams every night. But Adam saw only Cat.

Issa took a deep breath outside Diego's study, wiping the tears off her cheeks. Last time, she promised herself. Last time Cat would ever see her cry.

She pushed the door of the study open silently. Her mother sat in Diego's high-backed chair, holding a cell phone to her ear. Issa could hear the conversation clearly in the well-insulated room.

"Roy is not coming back, Helen. I'm sorry this is hard for you to face, but it's a fact. The man has been gone for five years now."

Strict Aunt Helen. Her father's sister was convinced something terrible had happened to Roy Bradley and he would magically appear one day. Issa wished with all her heart that was true.

After a silence, Alisha sighed. "I am marrying Diego. And that's it. I've been divorced for—"

Issa could hear the voice on the other end of the cell phone growing more insistent.

"Diego will be good for Issa. He's kind and generous and— Helen, please. She's my daughter and I am doing the best I can for her."

"Mom?"

Alisha whirled around, her cheeks coloring.

"Give me the phone." Issa held out her hand.

Alisha hesitated.

"Let me talk to her. Please."

Alisha handed over the cell, her expression defeated.

"Auntie Helen. It's Iz."

"What is she doing to you?" Issa could hear Aunt Helen sobbing. "Marrying some ignorant spic when your father is looking for you? Don't worry, child. You come and stay with us. We'll take care of you and—"

"Please listen to me?"

"Child." Helen was quiet after that.

Issa glanced at Alisha. Her mother was staring at her hands, twisting her engagement ring around and around on her finger. It was time for Issa to be an adult and take control of her life.

"Diego's real nice to us. He's decent. Real decent. And I know Daddy's not coming back."

"Child, you don't know that."

"He wouldn't leave me for this long if he was comin' back. You know that. I'm still your family, right? I can still come for Kwanzaa to see Jessie and Robbie and li'l Bo?"

Helen said nothing and Issa glanced at Alisha again. Alisha was blinking her eyes in the way she always did before she had a breakdown.

"Nothin's gonna change. I promise you. Please give Mama your blessings, because you know she won't marry Diego without them. Please. For me."

Helen continued to be silent. Issa started counting the

seconds. "If she wants to marry that man, fine. But, child, if you ever run into problems with them rich types, you take the first plane to Atlanta. You hear?"

"I hear. Thanks, Auntie. I love you."

Aunt Helen sighed. "You too, child. Too much."

Issa realized her eyes had tears, as well, as she handed the phone back to Alisha. For the past five years, being with her father's big, boisterous relatives made her feel like a part of his life still. Like he was on vacation and would be back any day. That would be over now.

Issa kissed Alisha on the cheek. "I need to do something." She rehearsed what she was planning to say as she trekked up the stairs to Cat's room. True, Adam might still be in there with Cat, doing God knew what, but it was time to call the truce.

I'll stay the hell out of your life. I'll get my own car and not try to take the Lotus away from you.

In return, you'll get off my back. You'll keep Adam out of my sight. You'll lay off me and my mother. Or I'll turn your father against you so fast, your fake orange tan will slide off.

That sounded good. She paused outside the closed bedroom door that could only be Cat's. A huge neon pink sign declared Entering the Princess's Palace. Prepare to Curtsy.

Issa raised a hand to knock on the door.

"I know!" Issa heard Cat's distinct giggle from inside the room. "You should have seen the look on her face. I just grabbed that ex-boyfriend of hers and practically jumped on him on the living-room floor. Yes! Right in front of her! She almost died. I'm telling you, Jewel. It was the single greatest moment ever!"

Issa's ears burned. How could Cat take so much pleasure in her pain?

"She ran off to cry to her mommy, what else? No, seriously. I bet you my stack of Green Day CDs that she's packing her bags right now. And if she's not, this is just the beginning. Wait till you see what I'm going to do next week."

Issa bit her lip, the tears threatening to return.

"No! It's a surprise. Let's just say, Miss Issa is going to never show her face at Athens again!"

Cat's laugh echoed in Issa's ears as she pulled away from the door. She had no desire to see what Cat was going to do next week. That was it. She was going to tell Alisha there was no way they could stay in this house. No way could she face Cat again. Issa willed her feet to move, carry her away from this place, but they refused. She stood, as if statue-ified, outside the door.

"Anyway, so did you see Rake today?" Cat continued to squeal.

Rake? What Rake?

"I know! Oh my God, he's so hot!"

Hmm, interesting. Rake…who was this Rake? Issa's foggy mind started to clear. Something told her this was important. She had to pay attention and remember this.

"I'm telling you, when I get crowned Snow Queen, there is only one guy who's going to be my Snow King. Rake Robinson." Cat sighed dreamily.

Rake Robinson. Not Adam Mitchell. What the hell did Cat want with Adam, then, anyway?

"Not yet, but I will soon." Issa could just hear Cat smile. "Adam? Whatever, as soon as I get this algebra midterm over with, I'll get rid of him. Daddy said if I don't get at least a B, the car's gone."

Cat was using him, Issa realized. Of course, she'd been so stupid. Cat was just using Adam. Not just to make Issa crazy, but also to get her work done.

"Whatever, Jewel! Adam's gotten a taste of me. He can never go back to Little Miss Kiss-Ass again. Do you know what he told me? That one afternoon with me was so much hotter than two years with her! I know!"

Though she'd never felt it before, that jab in her chest had to be her heart breaking.

"God! Have you seen her clothes? I snuck into the guest house and looked in her closet. It really is what you said the other day! Stuff I wouldn't even garden in!"

Issa counted to ten silently. Cat wasn't going to get away with this. No way.

Cat caught a fit of giggles over something Jewel said on the other end. "I can promise you, by the end of the year, Issa Mazum-whatever is going to change schools. And she'll take that slutty mother of hers with her."

Shaking with anger, Issa stepped back from the door. She was not going anywhere. Cat was going down. The war was officially on.

CHAPTER 7

*Sugar and Spice and Everything Nice but If You Mess
with Me You Better Think Twice*

Issa was in the school newspaper office at six the next
morning. As the people and events reporter for the Athens
Apex for the past two years, she considered the newspaper
office her only sanctuary in the whole school. Today, however, she wasn't there to write an article for the paper. She
had some serious research to do.

"What're you doing?"

Issa looked up from her tangerine iMac and saw Ishaan
standing in the doorway. She could ask him the same thing.
Ishaan covered the sports section and usually wrote his articles in the afternoons.

"Homework. What about you?" Issa smiled awkwardly.
She still felt a little stupid about their last conversation, but
Ishaan didn't seem even slightly weirded out.

Ishaan didn't bat an eye. "Couldn't sleep. Thought I'd

come in and finish up the article on the proposed rugby team before class started. So, homework, huh?"

"Yeah." Issa closed the LexisNexis search tool she'd had open. She usually used the site to dig up public records and legal forms on prominent members of the community, but today she was looking for someone else. Someone closer to home.

Ishaan dropped his books opposite Issa on the desk and sat down, looking as if he wasn't going anywhere for a while.

"So, what are you really doing here?" Ishaan pulled his laptop from his bag and set it on the desk, plugging the cord into the wall. "Issa Mazumder never sleeps without finishing last night's homework, so I assume you're not doing homework."

Issa's cheeks burned. Damn Ishaan. *Why* did he know her so well? "I'm looking into someone's background."

"For an article?" Ishaan stopped typing. "Who did you get assigned this month?"

"Not for the paper." Issa fiddled with the mouse.

"Okay, oh, mysterious one. What're you talking about?"

As usual, she didn't feel like keeping anything from him. No matter how crazy it made her seem. Issa glanced into the hallway to make sure no one was around before filling Ishaan in on the events of the night before.

Ishaan's eyes darkened with anger. "You can't stay there anymore. Did you talk to your mom?"

"No. I need to handle this on my own. It's my problem. My mom is just so happy that…" She shook her head. "I need to get some dirt on Cat. Something no one knows. And then I'll use it against her. I'm searching all over the Web."

Ishaan studied her, arms behind his head, front legs of his chair off the floor. "You're going to pull a Cat on Cat?"

"Exactly. She has it in for me, Ishaan. I—I need to do it." Already Issa could hear the desperation in her voice. She'd lain awake in her bed half the night seething with fury. She'd never hated anyone before. Alisha always preached that it took as much energy to hate someone as it did to love them, so therefore it was much better to forget hatred and embrace love. Issa was pretty sure her mother's tree-hugging ways didn't apply to Cat.

"Can I help?" Ishaan asked.

"Yes!" Issa was relieved. He didn't think she was crazy. Not that crazy anyway. "I'm using LexisNexis because too many results came up on search engines. Can you look through the Google hits on 'Catalina Morena' and see if anything looks fishy?"

Ishaan powered on his computer. "Give me half an hour."

Issa smiled. No matter what, he was an ace researcher. She knew she could count on him to help her out and keep it quiet. The last thing she wanted was word getting back to Cat.

They worked for twenty minutes before Ishaan broke the silence with a loud "huh." His trademark expression for when he was on to something.

"What's going on?" Within seconds Issa was peering over Ishaan's shoulder. "What did you find?"

"Something weird. Look at all the articles on Cat's father."

2000—Diego Morena gives $1 million to unprivileged children. 1998—Diego Morena wins libel case for Electronica Media. 2002—Diego Morena named employee of the year at Electronica Media.

"Yeah, so?" Issa skimmed the hits. Diego was a superstar as a corporate attorney at Electronica Media. He'd made his millions by climbing the corporate ladder and good investments. She already knew that.

"All articles start at 1995. Where was he before that? Literally, there is not one article stating any information on his life before 1995."

Issa scrubbed her toe against the floor. Nineteen ninety-five. She recalled her mother telling her something about Diego and Cat moving to the U.S. only when Cat was six years old. Ten years ago, that made sense. But in the millions of articles on Diego in the *Wall Street Journal* and the *New York Times*, there should be *something* about his life back in Cuba.

Interesting, interesting. Maybe this would lead nowhere, but she had to give it a shot.

"I need to do some investigating," Issa said out loud. "And I need to be alone in the Morena mansion to do it."

"Thanks for bringing me home, Mom," Issa said in her weakest voice. "I'm just gonna go lie down."

Alisha frowned. "You sure you're not dying? I'm sure I could call in a substitute for the rest of the day if you're dying."

Issa pressed a hand to her abdomen and unlocked the car door. "I'm not dying! Go back to work, I'll see you in the evening. I'll be fine and I promise to call if I need anything."

Issa waved and started toward the guest house with

Alisha still looking concerned. Issa knew why. In sixteen years, she'd been sick maybe ten times. Alisha always teased that she was Little Miss Unbreakable. Issa hated missing school for any reason.

But today was different. She knew the middle of a workday was the only time she could be assured that no one would be home. The whole house would be her own personal little LexisNexis.

She'd stumbled dramatically into Alisha's classroom and asked her mother if she could take her home. She'd claimed she'd had an attack of stomach cramps during calculus and couldn't even bear to sit in a chair for another second.

Issa watched from the window of the guest-house window as Alisha's Toyota pulled out of the driveway. She gave herself two minutes before sneaking out of the guest house and letting herself into the big house through the back door. She stood in the kitchen and listened for any sounds. Neither the Lotus nor Diego's Lexus was in the garage.

She had the whole house to herself. On any other day, she would have taken this opportunity to snoop around Cat's room and find out what Cat Morena was really about, but there was no time for that today.

Issa tested the door to Diego's office. Considering the value of the paintings and books in the room, she was surprised to find it unlocked. She quietly closed the door behind her and surveyed the room.

So many possible hiding places for Diego's secrets. The desk, in between the books on the shelves, behind each painting. Combined with the fact that she didn't know what she was looking for, Issa felt silly for a moment. So a

Google search had turned up no results on Diego's life beyond ten years. The Internet had barely existed before that. Was she just being paranoid?

Instinct told her to not waste time pondering these issues and to take this opportunity to start digging into Diego's life immediately. She tried the top drawer of the desk. A million pens, some sticky notes. Butter-yellow legal pads with Electronica Media letterheads with notes written on them. Boring.

She tried the other drawers, reaching into the bottom farthest corners, the place where people hid their deepest secrets. The most incriminating thing she found was a battered copy of the Holy Bible in the bottommost drawer.

Wow, Diego was secretly religious. Scandalous. She flipped through the Bible and a photograph fell out. She studied the black-and-white picture. It was a grainy shot of a woman. She had Cat's eyes and her long silky hair. Issa flipped the photo over and noticed two things. A key taped to the back of the picture with a name underneath: Maria Sanchez Soledad, 1994. Havana, Cuba.

Who on earth was this? Couldn't be Cat's mother, she had a different last name. Maybe she'd been a modern woman and used her maiden name.

Maria Soledad, who are you?

Issa sat back on her heels. Something felt off about this whole thing. Why did Diego have this picture hidden away?

She carefully pried the key off the photograph with her fingernail and looked around the room. Where there was a key, there had to be a lock.

Taking a tip from the old black-and-white *Maltese Falcon*-esque movies she and Alisha loved to watch, Issa felt around behind all of Diego's paintings to look for any hidden safes.

Nothing.

Hoping for a possibility of a secret room hidden behind the bookshelves, she started moving books out of shelves and waiting for a wall to start moving.

Nothing.

"I've been watching too much TV," she muttered as she replaced all the books she'd moved.

This was stupid, there were literally a million places Diego could have a secret safe. It might not even be in the house. She was wasting time. She should just take the first-edition copy of *Pride and Prejudice* Diego had told her about yesterday and go back to the guest house for an afternoon of reading by the fireplace. Now, there was a good plan. Now all she had to do was find the book.

It had to be expensive, so probably he'd placed it high up on a shelf hidden from burglars or unruly teenagers or whatnot.

She squinted through the sunshine pouring through the skylight to see the top shelves of the bookcases.

Strange.

She noticed there was a small area in the north corner of the library that had a shelf of books sticking out a bit. The books almost seemed like they were going to topple off the shelf. Issa dragged over a chair to the shelf and stood on her tiptoes to reach one of the leather-bound books. It came off the shelf easily into her hand. She reached into the empty space the book left behind to see what was causing the book to not fit. Her fingernails touched metal.

Interesting.

She quickly grabbed all the books on the shelf and placed them carefully on the floor. Reaching up into the now un-covered shelf, she felt a small box.

Issa wasted no time dragging the box off the shelf and placing it on the floor. A box with a lock. What were the chances? Pulling out the key from the Bible, she tried the lock on the box.

Perfect fit.

Issa sat on the floor and slowly opened the box, expect-ing a human skull or something.

No skulls, only newspaper clippings. In Spanish. Each article had a picture of the Maria woman from Diego's Bible picture. Issa racked up her limited eighth-grade Span-ish and tried to read one of the articles. From working with the press, she knew that the most important information lay in the first two lines of the article.

Noviembre 3, 1995. Habana, Cuba, Diego Soledad. asesinado, marido, hija, pierde.
Maria Soledad murdered. Husband, Diego, and daughter missing.

"Oh my God!"

Diego had murdered his wife, Cat's mother, and fled Havana!

Issa could barely breathe. She was standing in the office of a murderer. This explained everything. Why Diego never talked about Cat's mother, why Diego *Morena* seemed to only come into existence ten years ago. There was no Diego

Morena, only Diego Soledad, who was a violent criminal. A murderer who her mother was about to marry!

Her heart was pounding so loudly in her ears that she missed the sound of a car pulling up to the driveway until the engine stopped.

Crap!

She slammed the box shut with all the articles back in and replaced it on the shelf. She did her best to reshelf the books the way she'd found them.

The key!

She ran back to the desk and taped the key to the back of the photograph. She had just restashed the Bible when the door of the library swung open.

She looked up guiltily, her hand still on the handle of the now-closed drawer.

Diego stood in the doorway. Issa's throat closed up. He was going to kill her and bury her body under the swimming pool. Just like in *Desperate Housewives*. Oh, boy, this was going to be bad.

Diego smiled. "How're you feeling? Your mother told me you weren't well. Your mother and I are both taking the afternoon off to take care of you."

Issa's brain told her to move, to say something, to come up with an excuse for why she was sitting here in front of his desk. "I, um, I'm sorry. I came here to look for the Austen and I couldn't find it. I should just go—"

Issa forced herself to stand and walk as quickly as possible to the door of the study.

Diego placed a hand on her shoulder. "I'm sorry. I forgot to tell you where the book is. Let me get it for you."

As he turned his back, Issa prepared to run. She could run down the street and knock on a neighbor's door. She had to call the police. She had to warn her mother.

Diego reached into one of the shelves, his eyes grazing the shelf with the hidden box. Did he notice something off? "Here we are."

She had to get back to Athens Academy and see her mother in person. They had to run. They could never come back here again.

"Please." Diego held the book out. "It's yours."

Issa swallowed. She couldn't arouse his suspicions. She forced herself to smile. "Thanks, Diego. This is so nice of you." She realized her voice sounded high-pitched and terrified.

"Oh, you don't sound well at all." Diego's face creased with concern. "Please take the book and go lie down for a while. I'll call your mother and tell her I'm here now."

Issa reached out and took the book, keeping as much space between them as possible. "Thanks. I'll see you later."

"Please call if you need anything," Diego was saying as Issa practically ran from the room.

Police! Issa's mind screamed as she ran past the pool to the guest house.

Alisha's car skidded to a stop, barely missing Issa.

Thank God! They had to get in the car and go now. They would get the police. Diego wouldn't be able to hurt them anymore. "Mom!"

Alisha got out of the driver's side. "I called the guest house and there was no answer. I just wanted to make sure—"

"Mom! Oh my God. You won't believe—get back in the

car. We have to go. Now!" Issa was shaking as she threw open the door to the passenger side, earning a groan from the rusted Toyota.

"What the hell—"

"Diego is a murderer!"

CHAPTER 8

*Marriages Are Made in Heaven. But So Again Are
Thunder and Lightning*

"Have you been taking too much cough syrup?"
Alisha rolled her eyes, tucking a stray strand of hair back
into her waist-length braid. "I think you should go inside
and lie down."

If Issa hadn't seen the newspaper for herself, she
wouldn't have believed it either. But her mother had to trust
her. She couldn't go into the house with Diego. Who knew
what Diego would do if he discovered the truth?

"Mom, I am *not* making this up. I know it sounds unbelievable, but...I saw it for myself. In his study there are
these articles. About a murder in Cuba. He killed his wife!"

Alisha slammed the car door shut, her face setting with
anger. "What were you doing snooping in his study? Diego
very kindly took us into his house. You can't go through
his personal things!"

"Are you not hearing me! He has evidence in his office. It's in—"

"Stop this right now." Issa had never heard Alisha use that tone before, but once Alisha heard the truth, she would know why Issa was acting like a lunatic.

"We have to go to the police. Diego killed Cat's mom!"

"Diego told me everything, Iz. Let's sit down and we can—"

"What, I—I'll get the articles! I know where he keeps them!"

"On the top shelf hidden behind the books. I know. Diego showed me already," Alisha said in a calm voice.

Issa's mouth dropped open, her teeth still chattering. "What? And you believe whatever lie he told you? Didn't you see—"

"His wife *was* killed." Alisha cut her off. "But he certainly had nothing to do with it."

Issa felt a nervous breakdown coming on. This had been the longest day of her whole life. Frustrated tears squeezed themselves out of the corners of her eyes. She didn't want to hear Diego's story. She didn't want to live in a house with Cat. She wanted her mother back. Her best friend who considered her the most important thing in her life. Who was this woman standing in front of her defending an axe murderer?

Issa lowered herself into the open passenger side of the car, her head in her arms. She could go to Atlanta. Hide in Aunt Helen's house till Diego stopped looking for her. But what about Alisha? She didn't look as if she was going anywhere.

Alisha's voice sounded far off as she narrated Diego's

story. "Diego married a girl his parents found for him and they had a baby girl, Cat. They were good people. Happy."

"Just like ours was until *he* walked in the door," Issa yelled. "He is a killer!"

The Morenas' next door neighbor had just come home and was staring openmouthed at where Alisha and Issa were standing in the middle of the lawn and yelling.

Alisha glanced nervously back at the neighbor. "Why don't we go in the house?"

"I am not going anywhere except away from here!" Issa shot Alisha a fierce look. What was the matter with her? She was becoming more and more like Diego, not listening to her daughter. Where had all the equality in their relationship gone?

"Fine! Stand here and yell. When we get arrested for disturbing the peace, it's your fault!"

"Yeah, whatever. I'm sure Diego can get you out of jail. He has plenty of experience running from the police!" Issa was growing angry. If Alisha wanted to get into the middle of this, fine, but Issa was too young to go to jail for obstruction of justice. She had a long career in journalism ahead of her and she was *not* going to ruin it in the eleventh grade.

"Diego is not a killer!"

The neighbor quickly went inside his own house.

"Explain to me what—"

"Diego climbed the corporate ladder at his company, Three Isles Financial," Alisha continued in a lower voice. "He thought he was set for life. Then one day he uncovered a very large embezzlement scheme by his boss, Santiago

Sanchez, the CFO. He split the money with Diego and asked him to look the other way."

"And he did it." Issa didn't even need Alisha to confirm it. "That's the kind of guy he is, Mom. How can you even think of marrying him?"

"Diego was *afraid*. If he said no, he didn't know what his boss would do. He took the money and tried to figure out how to go to the police."

Issa was silent.

"Diego told Maria the whole story. Maria was ashamed of him and she went to the police with the whole story and Sanchez was arrested."

"Then Diego killed her."

"No, he did not! Maria was attacked and killed in their home the very night Sanchez was arrested. Diego found her body and knew that he and Cat were next. He took all the money and caught the next flight for the U.S. to here, New Joliet. And that's what happened."

Killed.

Issa felt her throat close. It wasn't what she'd expected, but she didn't care. Yes, he had a tragic past, but so had she. She deserved a chance at happiness and that meant getting away from here.

Alisha had tears in her eyes. "Issa, Cat has had a very hard life. She and Diego need us. That's why I think that we should get married as soon as possible. I trust him completely and I know he'll be so good to us—"

"Well, you're wrong! He's dangerous!"

Alisha had stopped listening, her face a snowy white. Issa turned around to see what she was staring at. During their yelling match someone had pulled up in their drive-way. He had gotten out of the car and was standing not even ten feet away.

Alisha hadn't moved, her lips still parted in the middle of a sentence.

"Dad?" Issa managed to get the words out. "Oh my God."

"I'm so glad to see you, girl." As if he were stepping out of Issa's dreams, Roy Bradley leaned forward and reached for her.

"Daddy?" Issa whispered again.

"I'm right here, baby. I'm right here." His three-piece suit fit his broad-shouldered body to a tee. He was clean-shaven with a fresh haircut. And as handsome as ever.

Issa felt her knees about to give as she felt Roy's arm around her waist. The guest house key fell from her hand.

"Is this the key for this place? Can I open the door? Alisha, is that okay?"

Issa glanced at her mother. Alisha had enormous tears rolling down her cheeks and managed a nod.

Somehow, Issa found herself sitting on the couch in the guest house, her father next to her. Her mother sat across from them, gripping the edges of the love seat.

"What are you— Daddy, where did you go? Where have you been?" Unable to contain any more emotion inside, Issa burst into tears. She buried her face in her father's shoulder and cried. Cried for all the years she'd lost with him, cried realizing this moment was real, and most of all, cried because her father was here. Now everything would be okay. Her mother would be safe now. Her father was here. Amir had been wrong, her father was back. Everything was okay now.

"I've been keeping tabs on you three for years. I knew after I left that I'd made a mistake. I also knew that your mother would never forgive me." Issa heard Roy's voice. It sounded so far off. She didn't even care what he was saying, she was just so happy to hear his voice again. "I want another chance. I'll never leave again. I promise. You have my word."

"Get out." Alisha spoke up for the first time.

"Baby, please listen. I had my reasons."

"I don't believe this," Alisha burst out. "You waltz in here, open my door and sit on my couch? Like nothing ever happened? You have a lot of nerve, Roy. That's all I can say. Now, get out of my house!"

Issa threw herself between her parents. "Stop it!"

Roy rose to his feet. "Alisha. Please. Let's talk this out."

"Out!"

"Alisha!"

"Mom!" Issa grabbed Alisha's arm as she took a step toward Roy. "We're in this together! You said! You have to at least listen to him. You have to do it for me!"

Her face red, Alisha gripped the back of the sofa. "Talk. You have ten minutes. Then I want you gone."

"I want you back, Alisha. I want everything back the way it was."

"Not possible. How dare you come in here and manipulate my daughter into—"

"*Our* daughter," Roy corrected her.

"*My* daughter. You gave up all rights to Issa and Amir

the day you decided we weren't enough for you. Go. Wander. Figure out your life. Because we aren't it." Alisha held up her left hand, Diego's ring flashing defiantly in the light. "I am moving on. With a wonderful, stable man who is willing to give us everything you weren't. He's taken in Issa as his own and—"

"I'm *not* his own!" Issa shrieked, but no one even glanced at her.

"Oh, I know all about Diego. His shady past, his bratty daughter? You're going to subject Issa to that? Can't you see she needs both her parents? Give me another chance, for Issa."

Both Roy and Issa looked with desperation at Alisha, who was shaking her head.

"Please, Alisha. I need you to do this for me. Remember that night you came to me and begged me to take you away from your parents? You said they were going to force you to marry someone else and you only wanted to be with me? We ran away to the D that night! I didn't ask any questions!"

"You expect me to pay that debt to you for the rest of our lives! You think you can just leave and come back whenever you want? You want to pick up like you never left!" Alisha's cheeks were flaming red.

"I got scared! I realized how tied down I was—"

"We were doing so well," Alisha sobbed. "You finally got that job you wanted. I finally finished school. We were finally doing well! Why did you leave?"

"I thought having kids would get rid of this Bedouin desire in me." Roy held tight to Issa's hand. "I really did.

I promise. Then one day I realized that we had put down roots. I was going to be there for a very, very long time. I just panicked. I needed to get away. Honestly, I was going to come back. I just needed to think about what I wanted to do with my life. I knew you would be able to support the kids. So I left."

"I got laid off from that job," Alisha whispered. "And we were alone. I was so scared. You left us with nothing. No explanation."

"Did you get my note?"

"A note?" All tears gone, Alisha narrowed her eyes. "Of course we got your damn note! That was an explanation? You leave your whole family one day with a note! And we never hear from you again?"

"I was scared I was going to ruin everything, so I ran. I traveled around the country doing this and that, but I couldn't forget you guys." Roy's caramel-hazel eyes were somber. He looked serene, peaceful and as if he'd done a lot of growing up the past five years.

"Daddy, why didn't you call us?" Issa asked. "Why didn't you call Aunt Helen and tell her you were back?"

"By the time I came back, you'd already sold the house and moved. You'd already gotten settled here. I knew it was over."

"You are unbelievable."

"I will never leave again. You have my word."

Alisha's eyes were going ballistic. "Didn't I have your word on our wedding day?"

"I'm only an idiot once. I had the best thing in the world and I lost it. I'll never do that again. Alisha, please. This is me, you know me. We're good together."

Alisha crossed her arms, goose bumps evident on her skin. Issa could tell she was softening.

Come on, Dad, she's almost there. Tell her you're sorry. Promise her you'll be there for her always. She'll forgive you.

Roy lowered his voice. "I wanted to come to you but I knew you would never forgive me. But when I saw you were engaged to Diego, I had to come. I can't let you go. You're everything to me. Can't you see that? I'll do anything for you. Look." Roy pulled out a sheaf of papers from his jacket pocket. "I inherited money and I actually did something with it. I bought our house again. The one in the D. Your brownstone. I got my old job back. Issa can go to her old school. She doesn't belong here with all these snooty people!"

Issa held her breath. There it was. A commitment. He'd bought their house. He was ready to be a family again.

"You've destroyed our family once and you won't do it again," Alisha said quietly. "I gave everything to these kids and you will not come here and ruin it. Just get out. It's over. You're too late."

"No!" Issa heard herself scream, and couldn't believe her voice was capable of the high-pitched screech that was rattling her vocal cords.

Alisha firmly placed a hand on Issa's shoulder and pulled her away from Roy. "Stay out of this, Iz. This is between your father and myself. He doesn't understand what a family is. He can't come in here and leave whenever he wishes. I don't want you in the middle."

"Stop it, Mom! That's not what I want!" Issa cried out. How had this happened? She and Alisha were a democracy. They were equals. Best friends. Issa had always had a say before.

Until Diego. Issa burned with anger thinking of him. A criminal. The day that Diego had come along, Alisha had decided to start using the mom card. Now their relationship was a one-way street. Alisha made decisions and Issa followed them.

"I won't give you another chance to destroy what I've built for us," Alisha was saying.

"He's not destroying us, you are!" Issa said bitterly. Her knees started to shake and she lowered herself into the couch. "How can you do this? We've missed him so much. All we wanted was for him to come back!"

"I never want to see you again," Alisha whispered in Roy's direction. "Get out. You haven't changed and you never will."

Roy finally stood up. "I didn't expect you would forgive me so soon, but I wanted to try. You're wrong, Alisha. I have changed."

"Just go." Alisha buried her face in her hands.

Roy turned back one last time from the door. "Bye, Issa-girl. I left my card on the counter. Call me if you need anything."

Issa raised her hand listlessly. *Don't worry, Dad. This isn't over.*

"I don't want you to talk to him again, do you understand me?" Alisha's tone was stern after the door had closed. She grabbed the card and crumpled it into her hand. "This is Diego's house and Roy is not welcome."

Yes, Mother. Whatever you say, Mother.

Issa nodded robotically. She was done trying to talk to Alisha. Alisha had stopped being her best friend in the middle of all this. She no longer had any rights to tell Issa what to do.

Issa slammed the door to her room, the first time in sixteen years that she had shut Alisha out.

If she won't end this, I will. And if that means bringing down Cat, even better.

Later that night, after she knew Alisha was asleep, Issa crept into the kitchen and retrieved her father's card from the garbage. This was not over.

CHAPTER 9

Loved by Some, Hated by Many, Envied by Most, Yet Wanted by Plenty

"Babe?" There was a knock on Issa's door early Saturday morning. The Mazumders had barely spoken during the rest of the week after the fiasco with Roy. Issa had made a point of getting a ride to school early with Ishaan every morning and spending the entire evening in the Apex office. Her list-making talent had kicked in and she had composed a ten-step plan to bring down Cat and get her parents back together. Some would say it was harebrained, but it was the only thing she could come up with.

"Iz?"

Issa didn't want to see or talk to Alisha. As far as she was concerned, Alisha had chosen her life with Diego over Issa.

"Issa, you in there?" Alisha knocked harder.

Issa barely glanced up from her *In Style* magazine. "Yeah, I'm here." She was still curled into the king-sized bed flipping through magazines. For her plan to work, she needed a whole new wardrobe and she had no time to waste speaking to a backstabbing mother like Alisha.

"Didn't you hear me?" Alisha glanced around the room. Issa had made a trip to Borders and had managed to carry home every fashion magazine in the store. Her room was now littered with *In Style, Marie Claire, Vogue, Elle-Girl...*

Issa knew nothing about high fashion and was thankful Gigi would be here in half an hour to help her out.

"What's going on in here?" Alisha pushed aside the current issues of *SHOP* and *Lucky* and folded her feet beneath her on the foot of the bed. "You going shopping?"

Issa barely acknowledged Alisha with a nod of her head.

Alisha's eyes flickered over the new picture Issa had displayed on her nightstand. It was the one of her parents when they were young. Alisha laughing. Roy kissing her hand. She wasn't going to hide her secret fantasy of having them back together anymore. It was a possibility. All Alisha had to do was look inside her heart.

"Hey, why don't we both go together? I need to get some new things too. Diego insists that we both need a day of relaxation. Why don't we do some shopping, then get pedicures, maybe get lunch at that new Italian place?"

Issa had full intentions of putting to use the credit card Diego had given her as a reward for her perfect score on the World Politics exam. But not with Alisha. "I'm going with Gigi."

Silence.

Issa knew Alisha was waiting for an invitation. After all, the three of them had had infamous girls' day outings in the past. There was the time they'd come home with identical bobbed haircuts and feather boas. Or the time they'd each pierced a second hole in each ear. But those days were long gone along with Issa's faith in her mother.

"Anything else?" Issa finally looked up when it looked as if Alisha wasn't going anywhere.

"Look. I know you're still mad, but I'm telling you this is for the best. Diego is a great guy. Look at everything he's given us."

"Well, if you say so, it must be true." Issa resumed reading her magazine.

"What's that supposed to mean?"

"Well, you're the mom. You make all the decisions and I listen. You've made it pretty clear that's how it's going to be from now on. Now, why don't you go and play house with Diego? I'm busy."

Issa ignored the hurt look on Alisha's face but after her mother left the room, she threw the magazine across the bed. How could she focus on platform heels when her conscience was yelling at her practical side?

Practical Side: Serves Alisha right.

Conscience: But maybe she really is doing what she thinks is best. After all, Dad did leave once. Why wouldn't he leave again?

Practical Side: She needs to give him another chance. We all belong together.

Whatever. Issa wasn't going to waste another second debating this. Three Towers Mall was waiting.

Half an hour later, Issa stood in front of a mannequin in the BCBG store, Gigi by her side. The size-0 figure wore a lavender top with ruffled spaghetti straps over dark denim jeans tucked into knee-high boots. The outfit was ridiculous. Who wore their shoes *over* their pants anyway?

"It's perfect for you," Gigi insisted.

"I'd look like Peter Pan!"

"You'd look hot!"

"I don't know how to look hot!"

"Can I help you?" A suspicious-looking saleswoman approached.

"She needs this in her size." Gigi gestured toward the mannequin before Issa could shoo her away.

The woman raised her eyebrows with the question obvious on her face. *Could this grubby kid even afford a pair of earrings from BCBG?*

Pretty Woman moment. Typical New Joliet saleswoman. Issa felt a tinge of offense. How dare this woman judge her? She had more of a free balance on her brand-new credit card than this woman would in her whole life.

"I have a lot to buy, so can we hurry this up?" Issa said in her most bored-adult voice. "I'm a size six."

The woman, still looking doubtful, found the outfit for Issa and hustled her into a dressing room. Gigi looked most impressed by Issa's new attitude.

Issa shook out of her Black Eyed Peas concert T-shirt and cargos and tried on the outfit. She felt ridiculous in the heeled shoes, and thought wearing such a low-cut top in the middle of the afternoon was just plain slutty.

"You *do* look hot!" Gigi sat, slack-jawed, as Issa twirled for her.

"I do not."

"You do! You're getting it. Actually, you're wearing it out."

Issa opened her mouth to protest, but Gigi was already at the jewelry counter, finding accessories to match.

Issa looked in the mirror one more time. Ridiculous, but definitely different. Very Sienna Miller.

Still wearing the outfit, Issa left the dressing room and marched up to the counter. Both saleswomen were glancing in her direction and whispering.

"I'll take this whole outfit."

The saleswomen exchanged glances and quickly rang her up as she flashed her American Express gold card.

"The outfit does look lovely on you, dear. We have a selection of purses if you're interested."

Issa rolled her eyes. Ah, what money could buy.

"Thanks, I'm good." Issa slid her credit card back into her wallet, earning a disappointed look from the saleswoman.

Issa fingered Roy Bradley's card, hidden behind her driver's license. She hadn't called him. Not yet. When she did call, she wanted to have good news for him.

Issa tucked her old clothes into the bag the lady offered her and sauntered back into the mall, enjoying the swivel in her hips brought on by the heeled boots.

Issa and Gigi got a lot more respect in the next store as Issa bought another pair of jeans, a black-and-white floaty miniskirt, some chiffon tops and a black shrug for cold days. Issa was slowly getting used to the idea that she would need to show skin and wear color. She started to think of it as playing a game of dress-up.

"So, what exactly are we doing?" Gigi asked in the dressing room of Armani Express. "I understand you need new clothes, I mean, I've known that for years. But you seem like you're on a mission or something."

"If Mom thinks she can become Diego and have me be fine with it, I'll become Cat and see how everyone handles it."

Issa slid a sheer silk tunic over her head and admired the way it fell on her hips. Very cool. Ashley Simpson wore something similar during her *Saturday Night Live* fiasco.

"What?" Gigi sounded disbelieving.

"I'll act like Cat does. I'll be nasty and evil and conniving. I'll make Cat's life such hell she'll beg Diego to throw me and Mom out. Poor brokenhearted Mom will go straight back into the waiting arms of Dad. And we're rid of the Morenas." Issa inhaled as she slithered into skintight black pants. Giving up breathing seemed to be a prerequisite for looking "hot."

"Okay. So let me get this straight. You're going to become popular and get Cat to hate you?"

"Yup. I'm going to take away the two things Cat wants most."

"Which are?"

"The Snow Queen title and Rake Robinson." Issa gasped out as she slid the pants off. Jeez, Veronica Mars could run around town and solve crimes in outfits like this, and so could the girls on *Smallville*. Issa couldn't even breathe and talk at the same time.

"Rake who?"

"Robinson. You know. The new guy on the soccer team. He's going to be my date for the Winter Ball."

"Huh. How're you going to do that?"

Issa had spent the entire previous week observing. She'd

sat in the middle of the crowded cafeteria and watched the various cliques of the high school. She'd watched the jocks act stupid because they were supposed to. She watched the punk crowd act normal when they thought no one was watching. She'd watched Cat be fake-nice to the new girl, then snicker and make up a fake rumor as soon as the girl left the table.

Issa had watched the small set of people who didn't seem to be impressed by Cat. And then she'd gotten an idea.

"The Belles."

"The country-club-perfumed princess gang? And you?"

"They hate Cat. We have stuff in common."

"Huh."

Gigi didn't sound convinced and Issa didn't blame her. To go from social mediocrity to the top of the Athens food chain took people years. But Issa had no other choice. This was the only way to get her family back together.

Their next stop was Express, which Issa knew to be one of Cat's favorite stores. After selecting silky camisole tops and fitted sweaters, she stopped next to a rack of pants.

"What's with those midget pants?" She pointed to a shelf of what looked like long shorts.

Gigi laughed. "Uh, gauchos? They're totally hot. Especially with boots like you have on right now. They also go really well with, like, strappy sandals."

Issa bought the absurd-looking, yet trendy pants and made a mental note: strappy sandals.

After a trip to Nine West where several heeled sandals and a pair of camel boots were purchased, both girls were exhausted.

Issa calculated her receipts. Already, she'd spent more money than she'd earned in her entire life. This was how Cat lived all the time, she thought as they stopped for an iced-tea break. She could get used to this life.

Until her mother left Diego and reunited with her father, of course. Having her family back together would be much more of a reward than these material things.

She gazed at her gorgeous new boots. But in the meantime, why not indulge?

Gigi insisted on a pit stop at the Clinique counter of Macy's next where Issa got her makeup done. As the saleslady finished putting on the final touches of blush on Issa's cheeks, she commented, "You know, if your bangs were wispier, it would really bring out your eyes."

Gigi's eyes popped open.

Wispier bangs, Issa thought as she paid for an entire makeup kit and a bottle of Beyoncé's True Star perfume. Why the hell not?

"Hey, Ishaan." Issa flounced into the *Apex* office early Monday morning. "Have a nice weekend?"

Ishaan didn't look up. "Yeah. Rocking. I was studying for my AP calc exam on Saturday night. Can you imagine what kind of…" His voice trailed off as he glanced at Issa. "What the hell?"

"Good?" Issa tossed her hair. She didn't blame Ishaan for being surprised. The rest of her weekend had consisted of a trip to the best salon in town where she'd indulged in a haircut, highlights and a manicure. The result was a flippy, Nicole Richie–like bob with copper highlights. Even though flatironing her ripply black hair had taken an hour and a half that morning, Issa had never felt prettier. She waved her sparkly pink fingernails in the air.

Diego and Alisha hadn't been able to stop complimenting her on her new look. Alisha had beamed as if all of Issa's new purchases actually made up for Alisha throwing Roy out the door.

"Really good. But what're you doing? What's with all this makeup and stuff?" Ishaan gestured toward her outfit. The lavender top with the miniskirt and black boots.

"Just working on an idea," she said, the nervousness obvious in her voice. She still hadn't been able to shed her self-conscious teenager skin yet despite her glamorous new avatar.

Next thing she needed to improve was her attitude. For her plan to work, she couldn't be the superscholar anymore. She had to be carefree and fun-loving.

She practiced a Gigi-patented giggle. "How's that sound?"

Ishaan gave her a strange look. "I'm so glad I'm not a chick. You sound insane. You don't even sound like yourself."

That was the point.

"Wish me luck. I'll let you know how it goes."

"I don't even know what you're doing!" Ishaan called after her.

"I'm going to become a Belle."

"A what?"

If he knew, he wouldn't approve. *Issa* barely approved of what she was about to do. It seemed to be fake and overly dramatic. Just like high school. But becoming a Belle was the first step to becoming Snow Queen. Everyone knew that whoever the Belles nominated became high-school royalty. Unless Cat Morena was in the picture. Issa would think of how to get Cat out of the way later.

She took a deep breath and swiveled her hips into the hallway and, ignoring all the surprised stares around her, marched up to her target: Serena Defontaine. The stunning brunette had lost the Homecoming Princess title and her boyfriend to Cat earlier that year. She was the leader of the Belle clique. They were all initially from the Deep South and considered themselves to be real southern belles. They were also infamous for hating Cat Morena and her little entourage.

"Hey, Serena!" Issa usually would never butt into the middle of a conversation in the popular girl circles, but she was now the New Issa. New Issa *was* one of the popular girls. At least that was what she was trying to tell herself.

One by one, the Belles recognized Issa.

"Hey, wow, you look great." Megan Simmons tossed her beyond platinum-blond hair and did the double take. Up until that moment Megan had never acknowledged that Issa was a member of the human race, although both girls shared the same English class and had for the past three years.

"Thanks." Issa did her perfected hair toss, as well, the butterflies in her stomach settling a bit. "So do you, Megan! I love that lip gloss on you. It makes your lips look like Angelina Jolie's!"

In fact, Megan Simmons looked nothing like Angelina Jolie. Her narrow lips and deep tan were more California beach bum than worldly do-gooder, but that didn't stop her from blushing and giggling.

"So, Serena." Issa wasted no time. These girls had the

attention spans of amnesiac goldfish. She had to make her move now. "I thought it was *so* awful the way Cat Morena stole Jason from you at Homecoming and then dumped him as soon as she got bored."

"Yeah, that girl." Serena narrowed her almond-shaped eyes. "She's a real piece of work."

"I know." Issa rolled her eyes. "I'm telling you. She's going to get it one day. She just did the same thing to me and, I swear, it's time someone brought her down."

Issa knew each one of them had had problems with Cat before. She pretended not to notice them exchanging glances as she opened her new Gucci purse and pulled out a tube of Juicy Tubes Beach Plum lip gloss, while trying to stop her hands from shaking. "So, what do you think?" Issa asked as she smacked her lips together. "Time Cat Morena got what's coming to her?"

Serena looked mildly interested. "Definitely. But how?"

Issa replaced her lip gloss into her bag and closed it with a snap. She noticed Megan Simmons gazing at the bag with envy. "I live with her now."

The girls couldn't hide their surprised expressions. "What?"

"My mom's dating her dad and we moved into their place."

"Really?"

Issa nodded. "Really."

This was going much better than she'd expected. At this rate, she would be a Belle by the end of the day. They must have really hated Cat.

"Wow. What's her place like?"

"Yeah, is she that bitchy at home?" Megan asked.

Issa smiled. "Why don't you guys come over sometime and see for yourself? Cat's casa is su casa."

"Oh." Serena looked around at the circle of Belles. "Seriously? That sounds great. When's a good time?"

"How about this afternoon? I'll e-mail you guys the address." With that Issa spun on her heeled shoe and cat-walked down the hallway.

Whew. Act I complete. She felt like she deserved an Oscar for her superconfident socialite attitude. Or at least a Golden Globe. She had to work extra hard to keep all traces of her old self out of the conversation.

"Whoa, that was amazing!" Gigi caught Issa's arm in the band hallway. "Those Belles looked shocked! And by the way, six guys have come up to me and asked who the new girl is. None of them can believe it's little Issa Mazumder. You're like a movie star!"

"I feel like a different person. Call me Isabelle from now on. Get it? 'Belle'?"

"Isabelle," Gigi repeated. *"Trés chic."*

"Exactly."

Issa parted her lips and turned her gaze on a dazed-looking freshman who stood frozen at the water fountain. She rewarded him with a smile and he managed a goofy grin back.

Timid, pushover Issa was dead. Isabelle was born and she was someone Cat Morena would have a hell of a time reckoning with.

CHAPTER 10

*A Lie Gets Halfway Around the World Before the Truth
Has a Chance to Get its Pants On*

"**This** place is bigger than J. Lo's Miami beach house!"
Megan Simmons was awestruck as she and Serena got the
grand tour of the Morena mansion.

"Diego's not home, is he?" Serena whispered.

"Yeah," Megan chimed in. "I hear he's like a drug dealer
or something."

Issa smiled. Ah, the Athens rumor mill. "No comment."
She led the girls into the fancy living room, the same room
Cat had been making out with Adam in.

"So, tell me how this happened, Isabelle." Serena
plopped down into a leather ottoman. "How did you get
into the inner life of Cat Morena?"

Issa was still trying to get used to being called the name
of her alter ego: Isabelle. Beautiful, vivacious Isabelle. So
different from the meek and accepting Issa Mazumder.

"Well, my mom had Cat in her Intro to Oils class and

apparently Cat was failing or something," Issa embellished. "Mom had to call Diego, Cat's dad. He fell in love with her, proposed and here we are."

"So you and Cat," Megan Simmons said, finally focused on the conversation, "are going to be stepsisters?"

Not if I have anything to say about it.

"Looks that way," Issa voiced. "Interesting, right?"

"Yeah. Interesting," Serena said. "So, about what you were saying. You're going to bring down Cat. Even though she's going to be your stepsister?"

When Serena said it like that, it sounded downright cold. But what Serena didn't know was that Cat Morena would never be Issa's sister.

"She needs to be brought down a notch, don't you think?" Issa covered smoothly. Let the Belles think what they wanted for a while.

Serena studied Issa's face. "What are you thinking?"

Issa tested the waters. "Snow Queen of the Winter Ball." Issa tested the waters.

"What about it?"

"That's what Cat wants to be."

Serena rolled her eyes. "It's not going to be much of a competition. I have no desire to even think about it. After the Homecoming Princess fiasco, well, you know, I don't want to waste any more energy on that. None of the other Belles want to have anything to do with these contests any-more either. Cat plays dirty."

Issa smiled. "I'm going to play dirtier. And I need you guys to be on my side when this goes down."

She'd been practicing that line all morning in her head. It sounded even better than she'd thought it would.

"What're you going to—" Serena started to ask.

"We're totally there." Megan spoke up. "Cat and I used to be friends our freshman year. One day she and I were tanning out by the pool instead of going to gym class, and I told her I had a thing for Laurent. You remember, that hot French transfer student."

Issa nodded. She had a pretty good feeling where this story was going. There seemed to be a common thread. Girl liked boy. Cat found out. Cat went after and got boy. No wonder she had so many enemies.

"Well, three weeks later, I caught them together in the gym behind the bleachers." Megan's nut-colored skin was practically turning purple. "And she'd asked me there to practice some new cheers. She wanted me to find them together!"

Issa gave Megan her best sympathetic smile. "I'm so sorry, that must have been awful! I really thought you and Laurent would have been so great together. You were almost like soul mates!"

Issa knew she was laying it on thick, but Megan wasn't exactly known as the sharpest knife in the drawer.

Serena watched this little exchange with a tiny smile on her lips and Issa realized she wasn't fooling her one bit. Serena was smarter than Issa expected. Maybe it wouldn't be that easy to become a Belle.

The front door slammed and Cat's stiletto heels could be heard tapping through the front hallway. *"Hola, Papi!"*

"We're in here, Cat!" Issa called, neglecting to mention who the "we" were.

Serena raised her eyebrows at Megan just as Cat materialized at the door of the living room, the smile vanishing off her face. "Why are you guys in my house?"

"Now, now. Be nice," Issa admonished Cat with a swoosh of bouncy hair. "Megan and Serena are my guests."

Cat did a double take. "What the— Issa! You look—" Her shocked look was replaced by a conniving smile. "Wasted no time spending my dad's money, huh, *chica?* So, how'd you manage it?"

Issa fingered the bill of her new newsboy cap. "All gifts from Diego. I did fantastically in World Politics and he was very impressed. He said he'd never seen such high grades in this house before."

Megan started to giggle at the furious look on Cat's face. Issa joined her and even Serena contributed a tight smile.

"Get out of my house! All of you!" Cat's cheeks started to burn up.

"Is that any way to talk to your soon-to-be stepsister?" Serena asked sweetly.

Cat's eyes darted to each girl. "You guys have nothing else to do than hang out at my place, fine. You *definitely* should get together and commiserate on how to keep a guy interested. Right, Serena? Jason says you need some work in that area."

Serena stopped smiling.

Uh-oh.

"Not all of us are shameless sluts, Cat. We'd rather be guyless than be after other people's leftovers," Issa said smoothly.

Cat looked shocked for the second time in ten minutes. Megan and Serena glanced at Issa with surprised looks of their own. Maybe she did have a bit of Cat in her after all. Being vicious was coming pretty easily.

"Whatever," Cat muttered, and flounced off.

Serena turned to Issa. "We're with you. If the Snow Queen title is what you want, it's yours. But you're going to have to deal with Cat."

"I have that under control," Issa said, a plan starting to form in her mind.

"It was good to meet your new friends," Alisha commented as she passed the chicken tikka masala to Issa. In honor of the Hindu new year, *Diwali,* Alisha had insisted that Diego stay out of the kitchen. That night she had prepared the one meal she had perfected, the chicken in a curry cream sauce, *pulao*—a rice dish with mixed vegetables and *channa* masala, a garbanzo bean curry.

"They're totally awesome, right?" Issa watched for Cat's reaction out of the corner of her eye. It was amazing to her how easy it had been to slip out of her old "downtown girl" skin and turn into this new uptown "like, totally awesome" East Coast princess.

Cat rolled her eyes but didn't say anything, as Issa expected. Cat wouldn't dare bad-mouth her almost sister's new friends in front of Diego.

"Catalina always has her friends—Sunshine and Jewel, is it?—over, as well. Perhaps one day, all of you can spend time together." Diego took a bite of rice and chicken curry. "Alisha, I will dream of this cooking tonight. You are, as always, amazing."

Alisha blushed.

Issa nearly gagged. Everything seemed normal until Diego made a comment like that and Issa realized how desperately she missed her father. She thought of her father's card, still hidden in her wallet. She would call him tonight and wish him a happy *Diwali*. Even though he wasn't Indian, he loved celebrating the "Festival of Lights." He was always the first one to bust out the illegal fireworks.

"Issa, what do you think?" Diego asked her. "Would you like to have a girls' night with your friends and Cat's friends? Perhaps next weekend?"

Cat scoffed, earning a sharp look from her father.

Issa stopped chewing. Suddenly she had an idea. Serena had made it clear that hating Cat and inviting them over to her house didn't make Issa a Belle. The only way into the clique was a drastic measure. Something the other Belles hadn't been able to do.

Something like taking away Cat's active social life.

Something Serena had said popped into her head.

Sunshine and Jewel are about as intelligent as boxes of hair. They're probably doing serious illegal stuff in their powder-pink bedrooms.

Hmm, so what if it was just a speculation? Diego had full rights to hear what kinds of people his daughter hung out with.

"I would love to hang with Sunshine and Jewel sometime, Cat. I mean, I don't believe a word of those glue-sniffing rumors!" Issa gave Cat her sweetest smile.

Alisha looked curiously at Issa. "Glue-sniffing rumors?"

"What the hell—" Cat's fork clattered to the table.

"Cat's friends?" Diego's voice could have cut glass.

Issa pretended to shift nervously in her seat. "I don't know if it's any of my business to tell. I mean, they are just rumors, and—"

"You're such a lying bitch!" Cat clenched her fist around a glass of water. "*Papi,* do not listen to—"

"Catalina Santiago Morena! New house rule! We *never* use that kind of language in this house. Do you understand me?"

"*Papi!*"

"Not another word! I want to hear what Issa has to say."

"Maybe I should go." Issa pretended to hesitantly stand up. "You guys should talk."

"Please tell me, Issa. *Por favor.* You two are going to be sisters. If Catalina has fallen in with a bad crowd, I—"

Issa glanced from Diego to Cat to Alisha. Alisha had a look of concern on her face. Issa had to force herself to not smirk. She was getting good. Not even her own mother could tell she was totally making this up as she went.

"Well, Cat's friends, Sunshine, Jewel, some of the guys. Well, everyone says that they—you know, they...do illegal stuff."

Alisha bit her lip. "Cat, do you know about this?"

"*My friends do not do drugs! And neither do I!*" Cat screeched loudly enough to cause the chandelier to sway. Light beams from the heavy chandelier bounced around the room and landed squarely on Cat, like a spotlight.

"Well, I don't think Cat does drugs, and these are just rumors," Issa said hastily. She didn't want to push it. Knowing Diego, he would drag Cat to do a drug test in the morning and this whole lie would be over.

Cat looked deadly furious, like a villainess on TV. Her cheeks blazed and her eyes were the color of emeralds.

"I don't want to say anymore." Issa lowered her eyes demurely. "But remember the weekend before you guys announced your engagement news to us? Cat threw a party here that weekend. Who knows what her friends were doing in this house?"

"*Papi,* she is lying to you!"

Diego's face was ashen. "Was there a party? I can find out from the neighbors, you know that."

Silence in the room. Issa glanced at Alisha. Now her mother would hear the truth.

"Papi, *please listen!*"

"*Was there a party here that weekend? Yes or no!*"

"Just a small one, *Papi,* and—"

A vein in Diego's forehead was throbbing. "This is unbelievable. I expected far more from my daughter. I've taught her better than this!"

"Diego—" Alisha spoke up.

Fuming, he threw his napkin on the table. "First her low grades, these wild parties, then these drug-addict friends? I've had enough. Cat is going to transfer schools."

This was *not* going as planned. Issa almost opened her mouth to tell Diego that maybe she was speaking too soon. For her plan to work, Cat had to be at Athens and watch Issa's game play out.

"Diego, please." Alisha stood up too. "Cat's made a mistake. I think with some guidance, she can leave behind these friends of hers and improve her grades. Perhaps some discipline might be better than any drastic measures."

Alisha turned to Cat and motioned toward Diego. *Apologize. Now,* her mother's expression seemed to say.

Cat glared spitefully at Alisha and turned her fierce eyes on Issa.

Issa looked back at Cat squarely, no fear, no hesitation. *You're finally getting what you deserve.*

"I expected you to be a good student, follow rules and not get into trouble. You're going down the wrong path!" Diego looked as if he might cry. "How can you do this, Catalina?"

Issa watched this whole scene with interest. Despite Diego's enormous love for his daughter, he was paranoid. He was so afraid she would go down his path, one of breaking the law and spending his life in regret.

She could use this.

"*Papi,* I haven't done anything wrong."

"How many lies have you told me?" Diego was shaking his head. Suddenly, he didn't look like Antonio Banderas anymore. He looked old, and very tired.

Issa felt an unsettling in her stomach. Despite everything, she had to admit Diego had been good to her. He trusted her with his house, his cars and even his daughter's life. Now she was breaking that trust to further her own goals.

This wasn't her. This wasn't the kind of person her father would want her to be. Not even for his sake.

"Catalina, I haven't been strict with you and I see what has happened. Everything will change from this moment on."

"What do you mean, *Papi?*"

Issa watched as Cat's eyes filled with tears. Cat was one of those annoying people who looked especially beautiful when she cried. Her huge green eyes pooled with glistening tears, her eyelashes darkened and her pouty lips trembled. Issa sighed. Unfair. No matter how unfortunate Cat's situation got, she was still a stunner. When Issa cried, she was a red, blotchy, snotty mess.

"From now on, you will go to school, attend class and come straight home. I will keep an eye on you at home and Alisha will watch you at school. You are *not* to associate any further with your Jewel and Sun friends. No more!"

Alisha stared at her half-filled plate and Issa watched the scene from lowered eyelashes. She hadn't expected the gushing guilt that followed Diego's statement.

Cat was crying openly now. "How can you not listen to your own daughter? You're listening to this girl over your own daughter? She hates me, can't you see that?"

"Issa is being a good sister!" Diego yelled. "You have a long, successful life ahead of you and I will not have you spoiling it for nothing. You are not to leave the house for any reason! No parties, no dances, nothing."

Issa cringed. House arrest. She would die under these circumstances.

"I want to see every single homework assignment you do and I will now speak to your teachers to make sure your grades are improving. If you do not do as I say, you will transfer schools!"

"Everything was fine until these people came! Now you don't love or trust me anymore!" Cat sobbed.

Issa felt another twinge of guilt. Cat really did look flabbergasted and Issa knew how it felt to be betrayed by a loved parent.

But for her plan to work, Issa had to play hardball. If

things had been reversed, Cat would have pulled this stunt on her. Actually Cat would have done far worse and she wouldn't have felt bad.

"*Nada mas!* No more car, no more late nights, no more shopping. You will go to school with Alisha every morning and come back with her every afternoon. I am not making jokes here!" Diego called as Cat flew out of the room.

"I hate you!" Cat screamed as she ran up the stairs.

Diego looked stricken and now his eyes looked as if they were about to spill over.

Alisha rose and lay a hand on his shoulder. "She needs discipline. This will work out, don't worry."

Issa silently pushed her chair back. "Excuse me," she whispered. She needed to go call Gigi and tell her phase one had worked beautifully.

"Issa, I need your help."

Issa paused in midstand. "Sure."

"I need you to make sure Catalina doesn't fall in with her old crowd. Can you do that for me?"

"Of course." Issa nodded. The plan had gone even better than expected. At this rate, her parents would be back together by the end of the month. Yet she couldn't shake the feeling that she was doing something she would always live to regret.

She left the dining room and decided to take a walk around the gardens. For early November, it was still unseasonably warm. The trees still wore their burnt-sienna leaves and Issa's feet crunched over the still green grass.

She traced her fingers over the perfectly trimmed rose hedges and sniffed a perfect white flower. She glanced up at the main house and noticed a light in one of the bedrooms. She could see a pale pink wall inside and a shadow of something that resembled a hunched-over figure. Cat's room.

As much as she thought she'd enjoy seeing Cat be miserable, guilt weighed her down. She was playing dirty. It wasn't her. This whole scenario of being a spoiled princess wasn't her.

She sighed. What a lousy *Diwali.* In the years past, she, her parents and Amir used to set off Roy's illegal fireworks and welcome in the New Year with good food, card games and laughter. *Diwali* at the Morena mansion had been a cold, impersonal dinner with screaming and yelling.

She trudged back to the guest house and grabbed Roy Bradley's card from her wallet.

After several rings, a deep voice answered.

Issa held her breath. Alisha would murder her if she knew she was calling her father, but she needed to hear his voice again and reassure herself this whole thing wasn't a dream.

"Hello? Anyone there?"

"Dad?" Issa said after a few seconds. "It's me."

"Hey, girl. How're you doing?"

Issa twisted the phone cord around her polished nail. Was there even an answer to that question? "Okay."

"Happy *Diwali,* babe."

Issa smiled. He remembered. He wasn't even Indian and he remembered. She loved him so much. "Thanks. You too. Mom cooked. Chicken and *channa.*"

Issa heard the sound of water running in the background. The familiar creak of the pipes. He was living in their old house. Issa's heart throbbed thinking of the good times they used to have there. That's where they belonged. She and Alisha could be there that very moment.

"I'm having Costco salad and bread," Roy said. "I miss her cooking. God, I loved that *channa*."

Issa laughed. "She's a terrible cook!" It was true. The family had lived on buttered pasta for years because Alisha never remembered if she'd added salt to a dish and always wound up overspicing everything.

"I know. I miss that."

"Dad, I miss you." Issa stopped laughing. She wondered what would happen if she ran away from here. She could pack a small bag and catch a train into Detroit, her D-town, that night. She could spend the night at their old house with her father. In the morning she would call Alisha and tell her where she was. Her mother would drive up to get her. She would see how happy Issa and Roy were in their old house. Maybe Alisha would change her mind and stay....

"Hey, girl." Her father interrupted her fantasy. "Everything okay at that crazy house? That Diego being good to you guys?"

That he was. Too good almost. It made her feel guilty every time she thought of how much she'd be hurting him. Issa nodded. "Yeah, I guess so. Just thinking."

"About what?"

"Mom, me. You. How much we miss you." Issa knew in her heart that Alisha still loved Roy. Otherwise why would she refuse to see him? If she didn't care about him, then it wouldn't matter to her if he was in town. It hurt her too much to be with him. She knew if she was around him too long, she would fall in love with him again. It had to be.

"You think we still have a chance?" Roy asked, his voice sounding far away and sad.

"I know you do, Dad. And I'm going to make it happen."

Issa trudged back to the main house and quietly closed the kitchen door behind her. Talking to her father had rattled her. Suddenly she felt like she was ten years old and her father was her hero, the one person in the world who could do no wrong. But, in her heart, she knew things had changed. That hero was no more. He'd disappeared one day with no explanation and this man who'd come back was a stranger to her.

She needed to see him again. She needed to know why he had left and what had caused him to come back. She needed his assurance that he would never do that again.

She needed to find Alisha and ask to go visit Atlanta with Roy to see his family again. Her father would need her by his side when he explained his disappearance to his sisters. She needed to be there to support him and understand the person he had become.

The main house was silent. Issa tiptoed along the central hallway, peeking into every room. The kitchen, dining room and living room were empty. She heard low voices coming from Diego's office.

"I need to know that you're here to stay," Issa heard Diego murmur.

Issa peeked into the room and froze. Alisha was leaning on Diego's shoulder, her hand on his thigh. "I'm not going anywhere, my love. I can't leave you. I promise you that."

Issa knew she should not be spying on such a private moment, but she couldn't look away. Seeing her mother in such an intimate picture with a man who was not her father disturbed her. She wasn't stupid. She knew her mother and Diego kissed and made out and did all that couple stuff, but seeing them together like a couple made everything all the more real.

"He's back," Diego whispered, burying his face in Alisha's neck. "Your first love is back. And he is ready to pick up things where he left them. You can go to him, give Issa back her family."

Alisha tilted her head to the side, giving Diego access to her throat. Issa heard her moan. "I need you too much. A young girl loved Roy very much once. He rescued her. He saved her. But that young girl grew up. The woman who sits here in front of you wants only you. Roy doesn't know that woman."

Issa bit her lip. Could this be true? If Alisha was really and truly over Roy, all the diabolical schemes in the world weren't going to work.

"But, Issa. She needs him—"

"I'll never deny Issa her father or his family. I want her to embrace her African-American heritage. But she's going to be a part of this family too. She has to learn yours and Cat's Cuban heritage, as well. We both do."

Issa shook her head violently. Not gonna happen.

"I need you, Alisha. I can't imagine a life without you and Issa in it. Raising Cat alone…I'm afraid. I'm afraid I've ruined my chance to raise my daughter as a good girl."

"Shh." Alisha pressed a finger to Diego's lips. "She is a

good girl. She needs guidance. Love. Support. She needs to know she is more than just a pretty girl with a rich father. She needs to know that she is worthy."

Was Diego crying? His face was still hidden in Alisha's smooth neck. "Stay with me always."

"Forever."

Issa looked away. Her chances of seeing her father any time soon were not looking good. The chances of her mother taking her father back were looking even slimmer.

"I love you." Alisha's words shocked Issa. She loved him? When had this happened? She squeezed her eyes shut.

When she glanced back, Alisha and Diego were kissing passionately. Diego wound a hand down Alisha's back and up inside her sweater.

"I want to be with you tonight," Issa heard Alisha murmur.

"But what about—" Diego groaned, and Issa backed away from the door. She did *not* want to know what was going on in that room. She'd been naive to think Alisha wouldn't sleep with Diego until they were married. The thought of the two of them together made her nauseated.

"I want us to be married as soon as possible," Alisha whispered. "I want us to begin our lives together. The sooner the better."

"You pick the date and it'll be done. I love you, Alisha. You make me believe in hope again."

Yikes. Issa turned and dashed down the hall as quietly as she could. There was no time to waste. At this rate, they would be married by the end of the week. She needed to hit Fast-Forward on her plan.

CHAPTER 11

I Don't Have An Attitude Problem. You Have A Perception Problem.

"Ishaan, I need you. Or I'll die." Issa dramatically threw herself into a chair next to her friend. It was the last period of the day and the last thing on Issa's mind was AP English.

"Holy dramatic entrance, Batman," Ishaan murmured, not looking up from his copy of *The Crucible*. "You ready for the quiz?"

They had a quiz on the play today, but Issa had gotten no studying done the previous night. She'd told Serena about her little lie about Cat's drug use and Serena had instantly called an emergency meeting of the Belles at her house and had insisted Issa be there.

Issa had retold the story with a lot of dramatic pauses sprinkled in, to the glee of all the Belles. The approving look in Serena's eyes had almost scared her. Serena really hated Cat. Maybe she was in over her head.

Five minutes later, she'd forgotten all about it, when

Serena had held up a hanger with a skirt clipped to it. A black tulle miniskirt in exactly her size.

"You're now a Belle. We support each other in everything we do. Welcome to the sisterhood," Serena had said. The other Belles, Megan, Jody, Jessica, Kristy and Allison, had hugged her and welcomed her into their clique.

Phase two done. On to phase three.

She had to find a way to meet Rake Robinson before Cat got to him, and this morning, she'd thought of a way.

"I don't have time. Ishaan, you listening?" Issa snapped her fingers.

"I am now." Ishaan set the book down. "God. You look like that Destiny's Child chick with all the makeup on your face."

From anyone else, that would have been a compliment, but she knew Ishaan's tone and it was *not* complimentary. She ran her fingers through her tangled coppery hair. Her slightly "nappy" hair was hard to straighten and even harder to keep smooth and flat. By the end of the day, her flippy bob had become a frizzy triangle. She made a mental note to make a pit stop in the bathroom with her bag of styling products after class.

"You know Rake Robinson, right? The new guy who just moved from Austin?"

Ishaan sighed. "Yes, I know him. We play soccer together. But of course, you already know that."

"I need to meet him."

"Why?"

"I just do."

"Fine. Meet him." Ishaan picked up his book again.

"*Ishaan!*"

A few students glanced up at the rise in voice. Little Issa Mazumder would never cause a scene in English class. Issa shrank down in her chair. *What am I doing?*

This was a very Cat Morena thing to do.

Ishaan seemed to think similarly. "I don't know what's gotten into you. Ever since you got this...this makeover—" he gestured in her direction "—you've been sporting some major attitude. It's annoying."

Issa felt as if she'd been slapped. She was supposed to be cute and funny, *not* annoying. She felt her cheeks starting to burn. Well, if Ishaan found her to be such a pain, she didn't need him. She would meet Rake on her own.

"Fine," she said stiffly, and turned around in her desk, fingering the unread copy of *The Crucible*. The first time she hadn't completed her homework. Oh, well, doing badly on one little quiz wouldn't mess up her GPA.

Would it?

Issa's paranoia kicked in and she started to flip through *The Crucible*. If she knew the beginning, the middle, the end and who got burned at the stake, she should be fine.

Cat wandered silently into class, a copy of the book tucked under her arm. She took a seat across the room from Issa in the front row and immediately opened up the book, not looking left or right. As Diego had ordered, she was arriving at school with Alisha every morning and leaving with her, as well. Issa hadn't seen her leave the house all week for anything other than school. After a few days of Diego answering all of Cat's phone calls with his scarily curt tone, the calls had stopped.

Issa glanced up at Cat in between page flips of *The Crucible*. Elizabeth Proctor accused of being a witch by a vengeful mistress. Was her fate really so different than what was happening to Cat at the moment?

Serena had spread the word quickly about Cat's "drug use" and subsequent grounding. The same people who had been stumbling over themselves trying to impress Cat last week were now whispering about her behind her back. The only person who Cat had been seen with all week was a puppy-dog-like Adam Mitchell.

Issa had turned her back with a swish of highlighted hair every time she'd seen them together.

Elizabeth Proctor...Cat Morena. Was Issa having Cat burnt at the stake just to further her own aspirations?

"Hey!" Megan Simmons flopped down into the desk in front of Issa. "You look hot. Those pants are *so* cute! I love them. Gucci?"

Issa nodded absently. Just being around Megan was draining her brain cells. A year ago, she would have choked laughing if someone had told her she would be making stupid chitchat with Megan Simmons. Unfortunately, for her plan to work, she needed Megan and the rest of the Belles.

"And oh my God, did you drive to school in that hot Lotus this morning? I *love* that car. I'm *totally* going to ask Daddy if he'll get me one for Christmas. Do you love it?"

God, last year she and Alisha had made a trip to Manhattan and seen *Bombay Dreams* on Broadway as their joint Christmas present. She could only dream of waking up Christmas morning and seeing a ribbon-wrapped car in the driveway. She always assumed things like that only happened in movies.

"I totally love it!" Issa summoned her best enthusiastic voice. "You should totally take a ride in it sometime."

"That would be *so* awesome. You are just *so* cool. I totally cannot believe we weren't friends like forever! Why weren't we?"

Because you people are too snooty to look beyond your Gucci-wearing crowd, that's why.

"I don't know, but we have to make up for lost time, right?" Issa offered instead, giving up on the book and setting it aside.

"Totally."

Issa suddenly realized a tiny would-be flaw in her plan to get Rake. What if some other Belle had her mascaraed eye on him? "Hey, can you do one thing?"

"Yeah."

"Find out more about Rake Robinson."

Megan's eyes widened. "He is so cute! Everyone thinks he's so hot, but he's so quiet! You're really going to ask him out?"

Issa shrugged nonchalantly, even though she had no idea how she was going to do this now that Ishaan was out of the picture.

"You guys would make *such* a great couple," Megan continued to gush. "Totally like Nick and Jessica."

"They broke up," Issa reminded her.

"Oh." Megan's face fell. "Okay, then like Ross and Rachel."

Issa squashed the urge to roll her eyes. Yeah, *just* like Ross and Rachel. Now all that would happen was for Rake to fawn over her for seven years, date her, cheat on her, get her pregnant and the two of them live happily ever after in New York City.

"None of the other Belles have a thing for him, right?" Issa wanted to make sure she wasn't stepping on any Belle toes. Stealing another's top-secret love interest was a major no-no in their crowd.

"He's still so new. We don't know where he'll fit in. Is he a jock? Is he a loner? No one knows."

Issa didn't give a damn. Cat wanted him and that was good enough for her.

"So anyway." Megan's voice dropped. "Me and the Belles were wondering about something."

Issa raised an eyebrow expertly. She'd been practicing the expression in the mirror for weeks. She had it down to forties movie-star perfection.

"Are you, um, black? I mean, you're so tan and your hair is kind of, you know…"

Issa felt her breath catch. Never had she been asked the question that directly before. She scanned the Belles in her mind. Caucasians. All of them. She could claim her hair was due to a perm gone wrong and her tan was due to an extended holiday in Cabo.

But she wouldn't. This whole elaborate scheme was for her dad and she was proud of him and her heritage. If being black meant she couldn't be a Belle, she didn't want to be one anyway.

"I'm half-and-half. My father's African-American. His ancestors are from Mozambique. In Africa."

"Oh." Megan's face gave nothing away. "Is your name really Isabella, or does Issa mean something African?"

Issa was ashamed. She'd never meant to deny her legacy, but that was exactly what she'd done by insisting people call her the more "sophisticated" Isabelle. No more. Issa was back, and she was even badder than Isabelle.

"Issa means 'our salvation.' When my parents got married, it caused a lot of chaos in between our families. My dad's sister, Helen, always said that after I was born, their family finally started to accept my mom. She said I was their salvation, therefore my name."

Issa's heart ached. And that was what she was still trying to do. Be the salvation of the family they'd once had. She'd almost lost herself in the process.

Never again, she vowed.

Megan was quiet for a second. "I'm black too, you know," she finally said in a low voice.

Issa tried not to let the surprise show. Blond-haired, blue-eyed Megan. Black?

"My real mom gave me up to my dad because he really wanted to raise me himself. She was black. From Trinidad. She was really beautiful." Megan didn't meet Issa's eyes. "The Belles don't know. All they see is my white father and white stepmom."

"I see," was all Issa could think to say. "I won't say a word, of course."

Professor Kidlinger walked into the room and started writing on the board. Issa glanced nervously toward the front of the room. Class was about to start. This was a really interesting conversation and she wished she was having it some other time, some other place with Megan.

"I always felt like, being mixed, it's kind of weird."

Megan paused as if waiting for Issa to tell her being mixed was acceptable. "Is it ever weird for you?"

Issa smiled. She couldn't believe she and Megan Simmons were actually having a real conversation, English class be damned. Megan had always seemed to be a superficial cheerleader. Issa had no idea Megan actually thought or cared about her heritage. "It was never weird for me in Detroit. Everyone just assumed I was completely African-American and I never bothered to correct them. When I moved here, I joined the *African-American Newsletter.* Everyone in the room looked at me like I was a wannabe or something. Like I was pretendin' so I quit."

"Do you regret that?" Megan frowned.

Issa tilted her head. "Sometimes. It's harder here to fit in as a black person at this school, but it's who I am. I don't go out of my way to tell people anymore, but I'll never deny it either."

Megan nodded. "The Belles actually think it's kind of cool that you're not the same as us. It makes you unique."

"If it's cool with the Belles, maybe you should tell them about you."

"You mean, tell them that I flatiron my hair every morning, and I don't really go to Desert Sun every weekend? That my tan is real?"

Issa laughed. "Yeah."

"Maybe."

"Look at it this way." Issa touched Megan's folded hands. "Mariah Carey and Tiger Woods are both mixed. And they are so amazing looking. And so are you. I think you should be proud of who you are."

Megan didn't say anything more. She lowered her eyes and turned around in her seat.

Issa's heart sank. She'd crossed the line. The Belles would be hearing about this for sure now.

"Tell you what," Issa heard Megan murmur. "You stop calling yourself Isabelle and I'll tell the Belles who my real mom is."

Issa glowed warmly for the first time that day. Maybe there was more to these Belles than just eye shadow and cute guys. "You got yourself a deal."

"There you are!" Gigi was waiting at Issa's locker at the end of the day. "I haven't seen you all week. What's going on?"

Issa grimaced as she stood on one foot and arched her other foot back and forth. Her four-inch-heeled boots were killing her feet. How did the *Sex and the City* girls walk around Manhattan in these all day? "Just busy, you know."

Gigi pouted. "We were supposed to watch *The Notebook* last night. You said you'd call. What happened?"

The Notebook! She and Gigi had a long-standing movie date every Sunday night and she had totally forgotten in her Rake Robinson quest.

"Oh, we had a quiz in English. Did Ishaan tell you? I had to, uh, get the book read," she lied quickly. Gigi would be furious if she knew Issa had ditched her for the Belles.

Gigi's face cleared up. "Oh, yeah, he did say that. He was so cute this morning, so worried about the quiz! How do you think you did?"

"Pretty good," Issa continued to lie. From the first page of the quiz, she knew she was going to fail. After a moment of panic she realized that she needed to worry more about how to meet Rake. A bad grade in English was totally worth it if her plan went as scheduled.

"So, I wanted to talk to you about Ishaan, actually. Did you talk to him like you said you would? He's still acting normal around me, so I guess he doesn't know I like him?"

"Uh." Issa had totally forgotten it. "Yeah, I did talk to him."

"And?"

Issa had no idea how to break the news to Gigi. Gigi was not known for taking bad news calmly. This could be a disaster unless Issa had a cleanup plan. A few scoops of ice cream with hot fudge would probably do the trick.

"Look, Gigi. I tried. I told him he was nice and you were nice and you guys should date. But apparently, he likes someone else, so—"

"Who!"

"I don't know!"

"You didn't ask?"

"I did! But he said, she was 'unavailable,' so I didn't know what to say after that."

Gigi went silent and Issa turned around to see what she was staring at. Ishaan was striding down the hallway looking purposeful.

"Hey, Iz, listen, I'm sorry about yelling at you. I'll help you. Right now I gotta change for practice." Ishaan didn't even look in Gigi's direction. "How did you do on the quiz? Was that the first time you didn't read the book for class?"

Gigi's eyes gazed at Issa with a hurt expression.

Oops.

"Uh, yeah, I'll, uh—" Issa hoped Ishaan would be able to take the hint and leave. "I'll meet you out by the soccer field, okay?"

She waited till Ishaan had disappeared around the corner before daring to face Gigi again.

"He likes *someone,* huh? You sure you don't know who it is?" Gigi asked quietly.

"How do I know!" Issa said, exasperated. "He didn't want to talk about it."

"God, it's so obvious! It was *so obvious!*" Gigi stomped her foot.

"What are you talking about now?" Issa rolled her eyes. She was dying to go out and see Rake and wasn't particularly interested in Gigi's theatrics so late in the day. And she *certainly* didn't want Gigi to reaffirm her suspicions that Ishaan had a thing for Cat.

"He's so obviously in love with you!"

Issa hadn't expected that. *"What!"*

"Come on, Iz. Don't act surprised. He's beautiful and smart and wonderful. Why would he like me? He thinks I'm a total ditz. Of course he likes you. He rescues you every chance he gets. You guys have known each other forever. Freakin' A, I'm so stupid!"

Ishaan having a thing for her? Right. After the way he'd spent the afternoon insulting her. After the way he'd kept her out of his life and told her none of his secrets. Right. Totally.

"Okay, now you're just acting insane. Ishaan doesn't *like* me. He's Amir's friend. He treats me like a kid sister."

"Whatever, okay. You lied to me and told me you were

studying for your English test. I bet you were with him. And you weren't studying!"

"Gigi!"

"Look, I don't have time to stand here and listen to you make up more lies. Thanks a lot. Thanks for making me look like an idiot!"

With that Gigi stomped off down the hall.

"Wha—"

Issa closed her mouth. She knew she should go after Gigi, but Ishaan was waiting. And so was Rake. She would have to talk to Gigi later.

Issa made it out to the soccer fields in record time and looked around for Cat, who had apparently become a permanent fixture at soccer practice according to Ishaan. If she caught Cat at a single extracurricular, she would have no problems ratting her out. Diego's orders, of course. But Cat was nowhere to be seen.

The team was already practicing for the spring season and Issa could see Ishaan, his mop of wavy hair standing out in the crowd of green-jersey-wearing boys as they kicked the ball around. He was agile as he maneuvered through the throng of defensemen and scored a goal.

Ishaan? Liking her? Ridiculous.

Issa put the thought out of her head and surveyed the team for Rake. He was supposed to look like Adam Levine of Maroon 5. Her eyes passed over a guy sitting on the bench by himself. He was lanky, but not thin, and had a smoldering look to him. He looked like someone who would be named Rake.

Very cute. Much cuter than Adam. Issa smiled thinking

of the look on both Adam's and Cat's face as Issa and Rake made their entrance at the Snow Ball. Cat would burn with envy and Adam would realize what a mistake he had made.

A Prada gown. Issa decided. Something similar to what Halle Berry had worn to that year's Oscars. She in a Prada and Rake in a tux. Pulling up in a limo.

The coach blew his whistle, jarring Issa out of her daydream. She noticed the team was milling around the watercooler.

Here was her chance. Exit Issa. Enter Isabelle. Issa closed her eyes and visualized herself winning Rake over and making him fall madly in love with her.

What am I doing? The only guy who had ever liked her was nerdy Adam and he dumped her for Cat. He even said she was ugly! The thought almost sat her down again.

I can do this. For Mom. For Dad. For us.

Issa made sure her gaucho pants fell just so over her boots and her black faux-fur coat highlighted her face and hair. She smiled as she approached Ishaan where he was talking to another player.

"Hello, boys," she said in her best husky Lindsay Lohan voice.

"Hey—hey, Isabelle," the other player managed to gasp out. Hmm, he knew her name and she had absolutely no idea who he was. So this was what it was like to be famous.

"Issa, this is Joe. He's the only sophomore who made varsity this year. Joe, my friend Issa." Ishaan sounded bored.

"Hi, Joey. You were really good out there." Issa did her trademark half smile and the words flowed out silkily.

"Would you excuse us?" Ishaan grabbed Issa's arm and steered her away from the starstruck sophomore. "Do you have to flirt with every guy? I thought it was Rake you wanted to meet!"

Issa did her mirror-perfected pout.

"Don't give me that stupid expression. You look like a fish."

Issa frowned. What was Gigi talking about? Ishaan didn't like her. Everything about her seemed to annoy him nowadays. Probably only his pledge to Amir kept him even speaking to her.

"Introduce me to Rake." She sighed.

His hand still on her arm, he dragged her over to where Rake had just strapped on his iPod.

Ishaan tapped him on the shoulder. "Hey. This is Issa. She's a huge fan of your work."

Issa ignored his sarcasm and rewarded Rake with her biggest smile.

"Hey." Rake removed his headphones and held out his hand. Issa slipped her fingers through his and gave a suggestive squeeze. She could hardly breathe. This was the first time she'd touched another guy since Adam. His fingers held hers tightly.

"How long have you been playing?" Uninvited, she took a seat on the bench and tilted her head back. She could barely believe she was doing this. She'd practiced in front of her mirror for hours and these rehearsed lines sounded almost natural to her now.

"I need to get back," Ishaan muttered.

Issa watched him leave and when it became clear he

wasn't planning to glance back at her even once, she turned her attention to Rake "Cat's Obsession" Robinson.

Rake was amazing up close. He looked much more like a young Tom Cruise before he got all weird than the Maroon 5 guy. His coconut-shell-colored hair hung over matching almond-shaped eyes, and the white jersey he wore set off a natural-looking tan. He had a tiny zigzag scar on his left cheek that was more Colin Farrell than Harry Potter.

"I've played since I was a kid. You come to lots of games?"

Issa threw her head back and laughed. "To see you? Always." She hoped her voice sounded throaty and sexy, instead of like she had a cold.

"Yeah?"

She shrugged out of her fur coat. "It's warm in here, don't you think?"

"Coach put in space heaters." Rake's attention was now completely off his iPod and he was watching her every movement.

"How smart." She raised her arms and twisted her hair to the top of her head and let it fall to her shoulders. "Listen, I was wondering. Do you want to do something sometime?"

Rake looked surprised by her boldness and Issa wondered if she'd pushed it too far. Didn't someone say guys didn't like forward girls? She could hear Serena's voice in her head chiding her on her stupidity.

"I mean, like studying. What classes are you in? I'm having a lot of trouble with English," Issa said hurriedly.

"Uh, yeah. Studying sounds really good. Why don't you put your number in my cell phone? I'll give you a call." He held out his RAZR.

Score!

"There you go." She handed his phone back to him, letting her fingers linger on his. "Have a great game."

She gave him one last smile before turning her back and walking away with her perfected strut.

CHAPTER 12

Everybody Pities the Weak; Jealousy You Have to Earn

Leave it up to us.

Issa reread the one-line e-mail from Serena and knew what her new "friend" was talking about. The sample ballot for Snow Queen had come out that day and there were three names on it: the Belles had nominated Issa. Cat had self-nominated herself. And Jenni Wilson, the school superjock, had been nominated by the girls' lacrosse team. Serena had assured her it was no contest. Jenni didn't look all that great in a ball gown and Cat wasn't exactly the most popular girl in school at the moment.

Issa couldn't help but worry. She *needed* that crown. It was the only way Cat would be driven over the edge. Cat would still win it, though. Not everyone in school knew who Issa "Isabelle" Mazumder was after only a few weeks of notoriety. Everybody knew about Cat Morena and her powerful friends.

She sighed and looked around the deserted school com-

puter lab. But that wasn't the time to think about the
crown. She had other things to worry about that evening.

Like school. As she'd expected, Issa had gotten a less
than stellar grade on *The Crucible* quiz. Her first C ever.

Professor Kidlinger had been so surprised that she'd
asked Issa to turn in an extra-credit report on the real
events of the Salem witch trials to compensate. Issa was
given a week to complete the assignment and here she was,
the night before it was due, with exactly one line written:

*The Salem Witch Trials were a travesty in the face of
American freedom.*

Issa Googled "Salem witch trials" and started sorting
through the links to see what looked valid and what looked
like some punk kid's useless Web site.

There should've be a law against future Snow Queens
doing homework on Thursday night.

Or any other night.

She'd spent every evening the past week either at the mall
or at soccer games with the other Belles. She sat at their
table at lunch and fawned over their outfits. Today her
outfit of an off-the-shoulder dolman-sleeve minidress had
drawn raves from the other Belles.

At first it was fun to talk about nothing more serious than
clothes, makeup and who was sleeping with who on *Laguna
Beach,* but after a while Issa started to wonder if she really
had anything in common with the other girls. None of them
had career plans except for fashion design and modeling
contracts. Issa didn't dare mention her journalism dreams.

"Hello there, gorgeous."

Issa was so deep in thought that she hadn't even noticed Rake entering the computer lab.

"Oh, hi!" Instantly she morphed into "Isabelle." Fun, flirtatious Isabelle who Rake had called on the phone three times that week. The Belles had made sure to spread the word about the new couple in town, even though they had never actually gone out on a real date.

"You ready?" Rake scrubbed his fingers through damp hair, shoving strands off his forehead. So far Issa had managed to not miss even one of his practices, but tonight's paper-writing session had taken her away from him. He smelled like an Amazonian rain forest right out of the shower.

"Am I ready?"

"Yeah, we're grabbing coffee, remember?"

"Right. Tonight. Starbucks. You have to try that coconut latte." Issa shut off the computer. She would pull an all-nighter and write the paper. She couldn't keep Rake waiting.

She slipped her hand through his as they made their way through the hallways and into the parking lot. She did her patented giggle as he talked about the goals he'd scored that day.

"I'm *so* upset I missed it. You must have been amazing!"

"You're giving me too much credit."

"Oh, whatever. If the rest of the team was as good as you, we'd be state champions by now."

Rake raised an eyebrow but didn't disagree. Issa usually hated arrogant guys, but on Rake, it was confidence, not arrogance.

She giggled again and leaned into him, enjoying how his broad shoulders just seemed to give off a raw, sensual heat.

As they approached the Lotus, Issa noticed a familiar car pull into the garage.

Alisha's Corolla. Issa frowned. What was her mother doing back at school so late? She hadn't told Alisha about Rake and she didn't feel like a scene at the moment.

But it wasn't Alisha that got out of the car.

Adam jumped from the passenger side. He immediately came around to the driver's side and opened the door for an emerging Cat.

Issa felt like she'd been punched in the stomach. He had *never* opened the car door for her. Now here he was, gently leading Cat out of the seat, his eyes big and love-struck as he watched her. What *did* Adam see in Cat?

Idiot.

Issa pretended not to see them, but watched carefully from behind her curtain of thick hair. What was Cat doing out of house arrest anyway? Issa knew Cat wouldn't cause a scene. All Issa had to do was tell Diego about her little outing and she was toast.

Cat ignored Issa, but didn't take her eyes off Rake for even an instant. Adam was, as usual, oblivious. Time to give them something to really gawk at.

Issa reached up and wrapped her arms around Rake's neck and pulled him into her. She leaned back into the Lotus and pressed her lips against Rake's, kissing him deeply.

She made sure to pull away first and gaze into his eyes. That should've done the trick. For both Rake and Cat.

Rake had a mischievous grin on his face and he reached

for her again. She gently pushed him away. "Let's wait till tomorrow," she murmured with a wink.

As she slinked around to the driver's side, she flashed Rake another smile and peeked behind her. Cat and Adam still hadn't moved. Cat's eyes were wide and Adam was staring at her, a look of horror on his face.

"Cat. Come on, let's go."

Gotcha.

Issa couldn't help but gloat silently as she peeled out of the garage. She officially had it all. Cat's man, Cat's car. The only thing left was Cat's Snow Queen crown and she was home free. The Morenas would be out of her life so fast, there would be skid marks.

A few hours later, the first snowfall of the season was in progress when Issa shivered her way into the Morena mansion after the coffee date. Maybe a minidress and Chanel pirate boots were a bad idea on a day when the average temperature had been thirty degrees, but Rake's appreciating glances had been worth it.

The hallway clock dinged seven-thirty.

She knew she was late for dinner, but the date had been totally worth it. She touched her glossed lips, remembering the kiss he'd given her before she dropped him off at his place. His lips made her tingle all the way down into her toes. She could hardly wait to be alone with him on Saturday night at the movies. She had a feeling they wouldn't see much of *Tristan and Isolde* like they planned to do.

"Issa, is that you?" she heard Alisha calling from the dining room. "You're missing dinner. We waited as long as we could."

"Sorry, sorry." Issa made her grand entrance and wrapped her scarf around the back of the chair before taking her place across from Alisha. "Lost track of time. I was studying."

Cat and Diego both looked up. Diego with a smile, Cat with a frown.

Cat had managed to get out of the house, take Alisha's car and miraculously get back in under an hour. The girl was a genius at getting away with anything. Those games were about to stop.

Diego passed the mashed potatoes smothered in butter and gravy. "You look very happy."

Issa could feel herself glowing. "I am. What about you, Cat, how do you feel?"

Cat's head jerked up from her meat loaf. "Fine," she said shortly.

"You didn't look too happy at school this evening," Issa commented innocently, hiding her smile. "Saw you in the parking lot."

Diego carefully set down the spoon he was using. "Catalina, you left the house? Did you ask Alisha before you left? You certainly didn't take permission from me."

Cat bit her lip. "*Papi,* I—"

"She did ask me. And I said it was fine. I even asked her to take my car and fill it with gas," Alisha said smoothly as she reached for the coconut green beans.

Issa's head swiveled. Her mother was lying. She knew the tone Alisha used when she was covering for someone. And right now she was covering for Cat.

"How's school going, Iz?" Alisha changed the subject. "Cat's really bringing up her grades."

With no friends and Adam as a boyfriend, that was entirely possible. A few more nonfailing grades and Diego might let her off the hook. Then Cat would immediately go on a rampage to bring down Issa. Her plan would be over.

Damage control time. Issa was ashamed of the thought that popped into her head. What right did she have to come between a father and his daughter?

But then, what right did Diego have to come between Roy and his family?

She had to move on with her plan.

"How did you do on that Crucible quiz, Cat?" Issa asked as she casually took a bite of her meat loaf. The quiz had been hard and she knew Cat couldn't have done all that well.

"I got a B," Cat said, a tiny smile on her face. Her face was scrubbed clean of all makeup and she looked like a little girl, with huge green eyes set in her pale face like a doll.

"That's much better than what you've been getting so far this year, right, honey?" Alisha asked Cat.

Honey?

Jealously burned Issa's throat.

Cat nodded in Alisha's direction. "Yeah. You helped me a lot. Um, thanks for that."

Issa clenched her teeth. Alisha was helping Cat study? Alisha, who hated school and had never once helped Issa? Did her mother actually believe Cat was family? Two could play that game.

"I got an A. I missed the 4th question, or else it would've been the perfect score." Issa felt herself nearly choking on the lie. She had never felt the need to lie about her grades before, and after all she never had a reason to.

Cat slumped lower in her chair and set down her fork.

"I am so impressed by these high grades of yours, Issa." Diego beamed at her. "A real scholar we have in this family, *verdad,* Catalina? You can really learn something from Issa."

Issa ignored Alisha's disapproving look and turned again to Diego. "Would it be okay if I bought a dress for the Snow Ball, Diego? I got nominated for Snow Queen this year!"

Alisha stopped eating. "You? Snow Queen?"

"Yes, Mother. Me." Issa didn't look at Alisha.

"But isn't that the kind of thing—"

Cat usually does?

Why, yes, Mother. But now a new princess is in town.

"It's not usually my thing, but the Belles thought I would be a shoo-in."

"I'm sure you'll be lovely," Diego said. "Brains and beauty are a very rare combination."

Alisha looked suspicious. *What are you up to?* her eyes practically said as she glared at Issa.

"You know, Diego, Cat's nominated too. I think I'll lose just because she's in the race!" Issa giggled.

Cat's face started to go white. Issa could bet ten thousand dollars, Cat had planned to sneak out to the dance without telling Diego and walk out with the crown.

"Cat? *No es possible.* Cat is grounded. She will not be attending the dance."

"*Papi!* This is not fair! I have been improving my grades. I have done everything you have said. Why can't I go to the dance? Why are you being like this?" Cat burst out.

Issa counted to ten while Diego glared at Cat. When it looked like Alisha was going to intervene, Issa spoke up.

"Actually, Diego. Cat's right," she said. Alisha and Cat both stared at her with surprise. "I mean, Cat's really trying. I think you should let her go to the dance. After all, she's going with Adam, who you liked, right?"

Cat stared at Issa with pure contempt in her eyes.

Issa stared right back.

Diego hesitated, looking between the two teenage girls. *Come on, Diego.*

Issa needed Cat to be there. Cat had to be there when she and Rake were crowned Snow Queen and King and had their first dance together.

"I'll think about it," Diego said. "If Catalina's grades continue to go up, we will discuss it. Catalina, say thank you to Issa."

"Thanks," Cat muttered.

Issa hid her smile behind a sip of water. "What are sisters for?"

"And now." Diego set his napkin on the table and stood up. "I have a present for my lovely fiancée."

The ring wasn't enough? That ring would easily have covered the mortgage on their old house.

Alisha obviously had no idea what was going on. She looked as confused as Cat and Issa as they followed Diego to the six-car garage.

Diego flipped on the lights.

"Holy crap!" Cat shrieked.

Issa had the same sentiment.

Diego shot Cat a sharp look.

"I mean, wow, how pretty," Cat corrected herself hastily.

There, parked right in front of them, was a sapphire-blue Bentley.

Alisha didn't react. Instead, she stood frozen, eyes glued to the car.

"It's yours, Alisha," Diego said helpfully, pressing a set of keys into her hand.

"Um, I—I can't, I mean—"

"I can't have my beloved wife-to-be driving around town in a car that might die at any time. It is, as Catalina says, an absolute piece of junk. I insist you have this."

Issa's throat burned. Piece of junk? The Corolla had been her father's car. The only thing remaining of him in their lives. And now it was being exchanged for an over-priced, vulgar beast.

"That's totally the same car Ben Affleck gave Jennifer Lopez," Cat added helpfully.

Right before they broke up. Alisha took the keys. "I can't thank you enough."

Diego lightly touched her arm. "What's mine is yours, *corazon*."

Issa turned away before he kissed her. Her father had his work cut out for her. Here Diego was, giving Alisha everything she'd never even dreamed of with Alisha sharing his bed for the past three nights. And her father was offering their old life of mediocrity.

Issa had to help him out. She had to raise the stakes and save her mother from falling further into Diego's world.

CHAPTER 13

The Only Way to Get Rid of a Temptation Is to Yield to It

Issa sauntered into the living room where Diego was engrossed in a taped baseball game and flopped down into the couch. She knew she was pushing it. House rule number whatever, no interrupting during baseball games. But she was pretty sure Diego wouldn't throw her out for breaking a house rule after all of Cat's shenanigans. Especially after the gift he'd given Issa earlier that day.

She smelled paint and noticed Cat sitting in front of an easel in the kitchen. Her eyes met Cat's and Cat quickly looked away.

"Is it okay if I borrow the Lotus tonight?" Issa asked loudly enough for Cat to hear. Cat didn't glance up once.

Moment of truth. Would Diego get angry with her, or would she be the exception to the house rule?

Diego muted the television. "Of course. You look lovely, by the way. That necklace goes very well."

Issa stood up and spun. Her outfit of a cream-colored

wrap dress, red boots and a red beaded necklace was exceptionally beautiful...and expensive. The whole outfit had been a gift from Diego for the A she had supposedly earned on *The Crucible* quiz. The pale dress perfectly set off her cocoa-colored skin and the heeled red boots gave her five feet three inches a major height advantage. She felt like a model.

Still no reaction from Cat. She continued to lean over the easel and scrape at the canvas with a stiff paintbrush.

Issa knew the dress was something Cat had her eye on for a while. Issa had seen the catalog in the trunk of the Lotus with the page folded down. Now one more thing Cat wanted was hers.

"You know I really appreciate all the gifts you've given me. You really don't need to do all this," Issa said halfheartedly.

According to Alisha, Diego felt obligated to give Issa these gifts because he thought he had to buy her love. Alisha wanted Issa to assure Diego she didn't need materialistic things to be happy.

Diego smiled. "Nonsense. Excellence needs to be rewarded. I'm so pleased you're looking happy. You know, Issa, when I was a boy growing up in Habana, I didn't have much. And then *ese diablo Fidel* came along..." Diego scowled. "Anyway, I want you to have everything I didn't. I want you to be happy."

For a moment, Issa forgot everything else and basked in the glow of contentment. She was going on a date with a wonderful guy she was very quickly falling for, she was wearing an outfit half the town had admired in the window of the Diane von Furstenberg store for months, and Alisha was happy. Was this life really so terrible?

For that one instant, Issa had everything she had ever dreamed of, including a stepfather who genuinely seemed to care about her. Maybe this would work out. She could go apologize to Cat right now and they could try to be friends. She could tell Alisha she forgave her and have her best friend back. The four of them could try to be a family.

Issa touched her beaded purse where she still carried Roy's card. This would all be fine if her real father wasn't waiting in the wings. Diego wasn't her father. And Cat wasn't her sister. And they never would be. Issa had to reunite her parents and bring her brother home. No matter what it cost.

"I'm going out with friends. Will you tell Mom when she gets back from her girls' night out?"

"I will surely do that. Drive safe, *querida*."

Cat whipped around to glare at them, but Issa was more curious about what Diego had said. "Queri—what?"

"It means 'darling.'" Diego smiled.

Issa's head was spinning as she left the house. How could Diego not see right through her? Her guilt weighed her down more than her faux-fur coat.

And the look on Cat's face. It was the same expression Issa must have had when Alisha called Cat "honey." Issa almost felt sorry for her.

Issa barely registered driving to Alejandro's Italiano Ristorante. She had always admired the European-style bistro from the outside, but when she'd seen the kind of patrons who frequented the joint—well-heeled, snooty, coifed women and tuxedoed men who looked down their noses at the waitstaff—she had known she would never fit in a place like that.

But tonight, as she handed the car keys to the valet, barely acknowledging his smile with a bob of her head, she felt as if she was finally able to play the part of socialite extraordinaire.

When had she become one of them?

"Why a frown on that beautiful face?"

Rake stepped out of the shadows of the pillars sandwiching the front door of Alejandro's.

Startled, she laughed. "Been away from you too long."

Rake cradled the back of her head in his hand and touched his lips to hers. "There's someplace I want to take you after dinner."

Issa's curiosity rose but she was unable to get any more information out of him over appetizers. She even did her patented pout and Rake laughed in response. She pouted more and he picked up her hand and kissed it.

She finally smiled and vowed to be patient.

Rake picked up the wine list. "What do you want?"

"Um. Anything." Issa was too embarrassed to tell him she didn't actually drink wine. Or any other alcohol for that matter, except for a sip of champagne at New Year's.

She wondered how he was going to handle the ID issue. Neither of them exactly looked over twenty-one. She found out a few minutes later when the waiter came over. Rake deftly opened up his wallet and held it up. The waiter barely glanced at it and took their wine order, a pinot grigio, without batting an eye.

Issa raised her eyebrow.

"Slipped him a twenty," Rake said in a low voice.

Issa blinked in surprise. "I didn't see a thing!"

"Practice."

Issa felt a twinge of jealously wondering who he'd been with the other times he'd been practicing. He'd obviously done this before.

With who? a voice inside her head asked.

She wasn't sure she wanted to know.

The wine arrived and the waiter filled both their glasses. Issa sipped the bitter liquid and tried not to make a face. A wine aficionado, she was not.

"So." Rake set his glass down. "Tell me something about yourself."

Issa traced the rim of her glass like she'd seen the girls do in movies. "Like?"

"Anything. Something no one else knows."

She pondered and took another sip to calm her nerves. A burning sensation poured down into her stomach and her head started to feel light. "I was terrified the day I asked you out."

Rake laughed. "I've never been so flattered. A gorgeous woman throwing herself at me."

Throwing herself? She hardly thought she'd been throwing herself. But she smiled and took another swig. "You deserved it."

Rake reached over and took her hand. "I had actually thought you were an item with Ishaan. I always used to see you with him."

Issa blinked in surprise. First, Rake had noticed her before? And second, she was always with Ishaan? "No, no, we're just friends."

Rake watched her carefully. "He was jealous when he introduced us."

Ishaan? Jealous? Yeah, right. At the moment, Ishaan was barely speaking to her.

"Enough about him. So, that's your big secret, huh? Your sexy girl act was just that, an act."

Issa smiled. "Afraid so."

Rake poured her more wine.

Dinner seemed to go on forever, and after they had finished their plates of ravioli *formaggio,* Issa stumbled out of the restaurant with Rake's help.

"I think—I'm so happy!" Issa heard herself slurring as she leaned on Rake.

"Let me take you to that place I was telling you about," Rake said softly. Issa blinked, trying to focus her eyes. The same valet she'd snubbed before seemed to be smirking at her. She held on to Rake tightly. Everything was spinning. She felt her legs starting to wobble.

Before she knew it, she was in the passenger side of Rake's car. So comfortable and warm. She sank into the cozy leather seat and let her eyes rest.

That was the last thing she remembered until she heard the car engine die. She sleepily opened her eyes. They were in a dark place. She saw the lights of New Joliet dotting the scenery below.

Lovers' Pointe.

"Baby." Rake was pressing her into the passenger seat. "You're so amazing."

His lips were everywhere. Her eyelids, her cheeks, her neck. Issa kissed him back hungrily. This felt luscious. She had never felt so wanted.

He kissed her for a few minutes before tracing down her rib cage and tugging at the tie of her dress.

Issa started to realize what he was doing. They'd barely known each other a week. It had taken her two years to get to this point with Adam. She wasn't ready. She forced her eyes open and pushed him away. "Not now. Not like this. I want to remember it."

"Baby—" Rake's hand didn't move. He loosened the belt and the dress fell open. His head dipped lower to kiss her.

"Please take me home." Issa tried to sit up straight, pulling the dress closed over the camisole she wore underneath.

"Already? We just got here and you look so hot. How about we just mess around? Not do anything serious."

A wave of nausea washed over Issa. She felt herself losing control of the situation. It had never been this way with Adam. When she said stop, he always stopped. And apologized.

Suddenly she just wanted to be safe and warm in her bed.

"I need to go home!" she heard herself cry out. "Take me home."

"Baby, I don't know where you live. Why don't we just sit here till you sober up? I'll just kiss you. Nothing more."

The car was suffocating. Rake's cologne combined with her foggy head. She couldn't breathe. She needed air. She fumbled for the door handle. She turned it and nothing happened. Why wasn't the door opening? She needed to get out of the car.

"What're you doing?"

"I want to go home, Rake. Now."

"Can you tell me where you live?"

"I don't—we moved. Now we live with Cat. And Diego, who's nice. But Cat's not nice. And neither am I." Issa realized she was babbling, but she had to make him understand.

"Should I call one of your friends to take you home? Does anyone else know where you live?"

Ishaan's face swam in front of Issa's eyes. "Call Ishaan. Ishaan will come. He's my friend."

Silence.

"Okay. I'll call him."

She opened her eyes and saw Rake's lips moving toward her. Then she felt his body press against hers, his hands separating the folds of her dress at the waist.

"Call Ishaan." Issa weakly pushed Rake away again. This wasn't the way she wanted this to happen. Not here. Not with him. This didn't feel right at all.

"Give me your cell phone," Rake said shortly.

She did so and rested her head against the window, trying to keep her eyes open.

After what seemed like minutes, she saw the lights of Ishaan's Jeep pull up next to her.

Before she knew it, the passenger side of the SUV was thrown open and she was in Ishaan's arms.

"Hey. Hey. Look at me. Are you okay?"

She gave him a sleepy smile and wrapped her arms around his neck. He was so comfortable. So safe. He would never hurt her. She could sleep right there. "I'm so glad you're here."

"Her car's still at Alejandro's," she heard Rake say. "I can take her home if you tell me where it is. You can get the car."

"I'll take her home," she heard Ishaan say. "What the hell were you thinking getting her drunk?"

"Hey, how did I know she can't even handle a glass of wine?"

"She's only sixteen!" Ishaan practically yelled.

"She sure as hell wasn't acting like it in the car!" Rake yelled back.

Issa felt herself slipping into a dizzy slumber. Ishaan's arms tightened around her.

"Was my fault—" Issa managed to mumble as Ishaan led her to his car.

"It's okay, Iz. It's okay," she heard Ishaan say as he carefully deposited her in the passenger seat. "Did he do anything to you? Did he touch you? Did he hurt you?"

"I don't—no—he didn't. I called you," she slurred.

"Why are you with him? Why aren't you with someone who loves you just the way you are?" Ishaan said to no one in particular as he pulled the car off Lovers' Pointe.

Issa stared at him. Was there anyone who loved her as she was? It sure didn't seem like it.

The car ride to the Morena mansion was a haze and before Issa knew it, Ishaan had fished her house key from her purse. "Thank God. Your mom's not here yet. She would kill you."

"Yes, thank God." Issa had no idea why she was thanking God. "Thank you too." She giggled. "Thank Ishaan!"

He didn't laugh.

"I'm going to carry you inside. I don't think you're going to make it otherwise."

She felt like she was floating as he picked her up in his arms and carried her through the front door of the guest house and into her bedroom. She kept her face buried in his neck. He smelled like *chai*. Real cardamom-ginger *chai*.

She hadn't had that *chai* in months. Alisha used to make it all the time. Now they only had Diego's Cuban coffee.

His prickly facial hair tickled her cheek as she rubbed her face against him. He was so strong. And warm. And smelled like home. Why couldn't they always be like this? Him taking care of her. No fighting.

"Ishaan, thanks," Issa mumbled as he laid her on the bed. She felt his arms release her and she reached for him. She pulled his shoulders down onto hers. She didn't want the feeling to end.

"Yeah, sure." He pried her fingers off his shirt. "I'll call a buddy of mine and bring the Lotus back. Don't worry."

"Wait…" She felt him stop moving. He was holding her hand. "Come here."

"What is it?"

She felt his breath on her face. She managed to open one eye and grazed his cheek with her right hand. His lips were just inches away.

"I love you," Issa heard herself whisper before she touched her lips to his, ever so briefly. An amazing feeling shot through her body and she wanted to do it again. Before she could, he pulled away. "I love you. Don't leave me."

What was she doing? He was one of her best friends.

"I wish that were true," she thought she heard him say as the door of her bedroom closed.

CHAPTER 14

When One Burns One's Bridges, What a Very Nice Fire It Makes

Issa glanced at her cell phone when it beeped in the middle of AP English Monday morning. A new text message. She reached to hit the read button.

"Miss Mazumder, is there a problem?" Professor Kidlinger frowned as she tucked a strand of brown hair behind her ear. "Would you like to share with us what is so fascinating on your phone?"

Issa's first instinct was to sink into her chair. She couldn't believe she was now one of "them." Annoying people who checked voice mails or text messages in the middle of class. So tacky. So pretentious. Stuff Cat's crowd usually did.

A Belle never gets flustered, a little voice in her head that sounded a lot like Serena whispered.

True. Her social life was *much* more important than *Much Ado About Nothing* or whatever they were discussing in class.

Issa summoned her best Belle voice. "No, Professor. Please carry on."

Professor Kidlinger sighed. "May I see you after class?"

Issa shrugged, ignoring the curious glances of the other students. Yeah, so she wasn't being her usual goody-two-shoes self. So she would get in trouble. So what? There were sacrifices to having it all.

As the bell rang dismissing class, Issa reached for her phone again. The message might be from Serena…or better yet, Rake. He hadn't called since their date on Saturday night and Issa was anxious for him to reassure her he wasn't furious for the fiasco she'd caused. Her memory was hazy, but she guessed she had humiliated him by calling Ishaan to pick her up and take her home.

Then there was the bit about her confessing her love to Ishaan and kissing him.

Thankfully Ishaan hadn't mentioned it when he'd called the next morning to make sure she was feeling okay. Maybe it hadn't happened. Maybe it had been all in her head. Maybe. What the hell had she been thinking? He was her friend, nothing more. And he hated her at the moment.

The text message beeped again and Issa hit READ.

It was not from Rake.

Iz:
Come see me on your break.
—Mom. Remember me? The person who brought you into this world and can take you out.

Oh, goody. What now? Did Alisha know about the drunken debacle?

For the past week, Alisha had been trying to make up and act like nothing had changed, but Issa had no desire to resume friendship with the shell that was her mother.

"Miss Mazumder?"

Issa looked up. The bell had rung, the classroom had emptied and she hadn't even noticed.

Uh-oh. Her chance to escape the surefire lecture had passed. Professor Kidlinger took a seat in the desk in front of her and looked like she was waiting for Issa to say something.

"Is something bothering you, Issa? You've been acting very strange this whole month."

"How so?" Issa replaced her phone, her heard pounding. The old Issa would have been trembling and shaking and apologizing. The new Issa would have none of that. At least not on the outside.

"Well, first of all, your less-than-average grade on last week's quiz. Then you failed to turn in the extra-credit assignment I asked you to do."

"Yeah, I was busy with school stuff. Sorry." Issa could barely look the professor in the eye. Did shopping and dating count as "school stuff"?

"I see. So, everything is okay at home?"

Oh, yeah, things were great. Her smart, handsome, virtuous father was within reach and her mother couldn't disentangle herself from the arms of a Cuban money launderer. How could things get any better?

"Yeah, sure. Things are fine."

"I understand your mother is getting married next month?"

Yeah…not if I have anything to say about it. "I guess so."

"That must be stressful. Your new stepfamily and all? Quite the transition, right?" Professor Kidlinger leaned back in the chair and seemed to be observing Issa's body language.

Issa self-consciously crossed her arms, covering her new pink sapphire bracelet.

"It's okay. Diego's an all right guy." Issa stared anywhere but at her teacher's face. She wasn't lying. Diego was an all right guy. And he would make some desperate housewife who could deal with spoiled brats like Cat very happy one day. Vivacious, full-of-life Alisha needed to be with someone who was a free spirit. Like Roy Bradley.

"I hate to see this happen, Issa."

"Mom getting married?"

Professor Kidlinger laughed. "No. I meant your dropping grades. You've maintained a 4.0 GPA the past two years. You're in danger of losing your A in this class. Have you given up on the idea of an Ivy League university? No more West Coast for you?"

Issa tried to maintain her calm exterior, but the panic must have shown on her face. Lose her straight A track record? Not possible! Her high grades were the key to getting into Stanford and on the road to her journalism degree.

"Losing my A?"

"Right now you have a B in here. And if you miss another assignment, it might become a C."

A C! She had never in her life gotten less than an A-minus. This was just not happening. Everything she'd worked for!

"I'll do better. Let me make up the quiz. Please." Issa

didn't even try to hide her desperation. Getting her family back together was one thing. Throwing her life away was entirely different.

"I gave you the opportunity to do the extra-credit assignment," Professor Kidlinger reminded her.

"Give me an extension. I just got so distracted by..." Issa was almost in tears. By what? Rake? Cat? The new Isabelle? "I can't lose an A in English. This is going to be my major!"

"Issa—" Professor Kidlinger sighed. "You were my top student up until a month ago and you've always done your work well. Because you're going through these life changes, I'll give you another day to turn in the assignment. Can you have it done by tomorrow morning?"

Issa nodded. If she had to camp out in her room till the paper was done, she would get it written. "Tomorrow morning. Thank you, Professor."

Professor Kidlinger watched as Issa picked up her Coach purse and stuffed her PDA/camera phone into the pocket of her quilted white blazer. "Please don't let the situation around you change who you are."

Issa's head jerked. Why did she get the feeling the professor wasn't talking about Diego and Alisha so much as she was talking about the new Isabelle?

"I won't," Issa muttered.

As she shuffled through the hallway to her next class, Issa made a mental list of things she had to do. "Isabelle" was going to have to go into hibernation for a day or two so Issa could swoop in and clean up the academic mess. She knew she was behind in her World Politics reading and her calculus assignments too. Looked like she was going to have to cancel her plans to hit the Louis Vuitton store with Megan and Serena that afternoon.

"Hey, baby," Issa heard a familiar voice call out.

She glanced up and saw Rake loitering in the jock hallway with a few of the soccer players. All of their eyes were on Issa and she forced her most flirtatious smile and lowered her eyes. One of the other players clapped Rake on the shoulder as he sauntered toward her.

"We're going out tonight, right? I hated the way the other night ended. I'm really sorry for what happened." He encircled her in his arms and pressed his lips against hers, his tongue gently grazing hers. His ever-present scent of aloe and eucalyptus permeated her senses and instantly, Issa forgot her never-ending to-do list. So he didn't hate her for Saturday night. In fact, he was sorry. He understood she wasn't ready to take that step. How could she have doubted him for an instant?

He was so perfect. Why did she have to call Ishaan and ruin the evening? She could have handled him.

"Definitely." She realized she was probably grinning like a fool, but she didn't care.

"Why don't I pick you up at seven?"

Issa hesitated. She still hadn't told Alisha about Rake and she wasn't sure if she was ready to do so yet. She would meet him wherever he wanted to go.

"Actually, why don't I just—"

Rake's eyes shifted into the distance. Issa glanced back to see what he was looking at.

Alisha and Professor Kidlinger were standing not even

ten feet away. They had overheard this whole little exchange. Neither looked pleased.

Crap.

There was no avoiding this conversation now. Issa quickly disentangled herself from Rake. "I'll find you later, okay?"

Rake looked more than relieved to leave the teachers behind as he hurried back to his friends.

Professor Kidlinger whispered something to Alisha and was gone by the time Issa approached her mother.

"You were supposed to meet me on your break, not be necking with your boyfriend," Alisha said shortly before turning on her heel, and marched toward the art room.

Issa tagged along, knowing she was in deep trouble if Professor Kidlinger had told Alisha about Issa's grade situation. Not to mention in deep trouble over Rake's little "finish what we started" remark.

Alisha closed the door behind them and took a seat on one of the counters. "Talk."

Issa looked around the room for a way out. She could vault from the window, but would probably break her knees in the process. There was no way she could wear a Prada gown and attend the Snow Ball with broken knees.

"Are you listening? Talk. Now. How long have you been seeing this boy?" Alisha's voice hinted that she was not above playing the mom card in about three seconds.

"Rake and I have been going out for a week or two," Issa said.

"Why don't I know about it?"

"I was going to tell you."

"When?"

"Hmm, how about as much time as it took for you to tell me you were marrying a total stranger!"

"You watch how you speak to me."

Alisha's sharp tone shut Issa up. Her mother was not playin'.

"Why did I need to find out from another teacher? About you and Rake?" Alisha moved easels from the corner into the center of the room to prepare for her next class. "Apparently the whole school knows about it. Apparently, you both went up to Lovers' Pointe on Saturday night and quite a few things happened."

Issa felt herself reddening. How did word get around? She didn't say anything. Rake wouldn't say anything. Ishaan? Could he have spread the word? She picked at a drop of dried paint on a chipped table.

"Nothing happened. It's just a rumor," she muttered.

"And when were you going to tell me about your C on that English quiz?"

"I'll fix it." Issa was starting to grow angry. "I've never needed your help in school before and I don't need it now!"

"You lied to Diego, Cat and me. You said you got a perfect score. Was that just to annoy Cat, or were you doing it for a new outfit?" Alisha grabbed a handful of paintbrushes and distributed them around the room. "Tell me."

Issa had no answer that wouldn't get her grounded.

"Where did this superficial Issa come from? Making Cat look bad in front of her father? Caring about nothing more than the brand of shoes on your feet?"

Issa felt the heat traveling up to her ears and hairline. "Me, superficial? You're the one that makes this crazy-ass decision to marry some random rich guy and expect me to just go along with it!"

"Do not raise your voice at me!"

What did Alisha want? She didn't want the truth and she didn't want Issa lying to her. There was no winning here. She wasn't the mother Issa considered to be her best friend anymore, that much was even more clear.

"You don't even sound like my mama anymore. I do not want to talk to you. Can I go now?" Despite her resolve, Issa felt tears popping into her eyes. She *hated* fighting with Alisha. Despite her new gang of friends and her popularity, she missed having someone to tell every detail of her day to.

"Issa, I am trying my best here to understand what you're going through, but you shutting me out is not helping. And these new friends of yours and this new boyfriend? I don't have a good feeling about this."

Issa crossed her arms. "And I don't have a good feeling about Diego. But do you listen to me?"

"We're discussing you right this instant."

"What, what do you want to discuss? You can do whatever the hell you want and you want to police my friends? There's nothing wrong with them!"

Issa's eyes fell on the clock. She was supposed to meet the Belles to discuss her Snow Queen–winning strategy. But Alisha didn't look like she was going to let her go anytime soon.

"What about your grades, then? How are you going to explain your sudden dropping grades? And then lying about them to make Cat feel bad?"

"Oh, this all about Cat, isn't it?" Issa sneered. Alisha

couldn't take her *own* daughter making her fake daughter look bad. Nice.

"Cat is behaving herself fine. This grounding has really done her good. Her grades are on the rise. Her attitude has improved—"

"Well, if she's your perfect daughter, what do you need me for!"

Alisha set down her paintbrushes and sighed heavily. "I think you need a change of scenery."

Issa's breath caught. Finally they were seeing eye-to-eye again. She did need a change. They both did. They both needed to leave here and go stay with Roy. It was the only way everyone would be happy.

"You're grounded."

"What!" Issa was sure she'd heard wrong. Grounding? How Diego-ish. Alisha didn't believe in locking kids up. Her parents had done it to her and she'd run away. She would never try that with her own daughter.

"You heard me. When Cat got in with a bad crowd and low grades, Diego grounded her. She's turning around. I think the same is necessary for you."

"Mom! Whatever, okay? You're not Diego. Don't even try to pull the parenting act now." There was something wrong with Alisha. Diego had gotten inside her head. He had bought her soul with a fancy new car and a comfortable home.

Alisha frowned. "I've had enough of this attitude. It ends here. No going out, no hanging with friends, no shopping. First thing I'm going to do is end this little game you and Cat have going with the Snow Queen. I'm going to remove both your names from the ballot."

"No! You can't do this!"

Everything she'd worked for. Alisha was taking away her newfound popularity and boyfriend in one stroke. And the crown. She needed that crown.

"This is for your own good."

Issa snapped. *Own good?* "Nothing you do is for my own good! It's for *your* own good! You move us into Diego's house. I beg you not to and you don't listen. I try to make the best of the situation and you don't like that either! What do you want from me?"

Guilt skittered across Alisha's face. "I want you to be the best person you can, Iz. No matter what the environment."

"Oh, like you're being?" Issa knew she was pushing it, but it had to be said. "You're scared of giving Dad another chance, but you're not scared of marrying some criminal! Why? Because Diego's rich? That makes everything okay?"

The clock in the room was suddenly very loud. It pounded in Issa's ears in tune to her pulse. Issa wanted desperately to get out. To run far, far away from all this drama.

"Diego is giving us a better life. Do you think if you weren't living in his house, you would be even thinking about this Snow Queen business?"

"If we weren't living in his house, I would have my father back!" Issa screamed. "Not stuck with a gold-digging tramp like you!"

Silence.

Alisha turned her back to Issa. "Go."

"Mom—" Issa knew she'd gone too far.

"Now. You think what you want about your father, but know this. I won't have you throw away your life. I'm watching you from now on. You are grounded. No more car, no more doing whatever the hell you want. It ends here."

Alisha was threatening her? It had come to this now.

"Whatever." Issa fumed and slammed closed the door of the art room...and came face-to-face with Cat, who was holding a large paint-splattered canvas.

Just what Issa needed at the moment.

Both girls just stared at each other for a second.

"Well, well, fighting with Mommy, huh, *chica?*" Cat had a smirk on her face that practically spelled out the fact that she had overheard the tail end of that conversation. "Seems like you're not Alisha's perfect angel anymore."

Issa would have ignored the jab, but her blood was really boiling. "Said the pot to the kettle."

Cat's eyes narrowed.

"Poor Diego, his little princess completely fallen from grace. Shady friends, disgraceful grades...where's your little entourage now?"

Cat bit her lip.

"What? You have nothing to say now, huh, *chica?*" Issa's eyes fell on the crowd of people who were gathering around. A few months ago, the situation had been reversed. Cat had humiliated her in front of this exact same crowd. She was going to take her revenge today.

"You're not going to get away with this. *Papi* is going to see through you and you're going to end up exactly where you belong!" Cat managed to spit out, even though it was evident from the tears in her eyes that she really didn't believe this anymore.

This was the moment Issa had been waiting for. Cat

Morena, standing in front of her, tears rolling down her cheeks, looking hopeless.

Issa laughed. "Please. You lose your father, your friends and your precious car. Not to mention *your* Rake can't get enough of me. Face it. I have it all, and, well, you're known as the town whore and meth addict!"

Issa thought she would feel jubilant as Cat reeled backward. She didn't. Cat ducked through the crowd. Alone. No one approached her. Even Jewel and Sunshine hung back, whispering as Cat dashed by.

She brought it on herself, Issa argued with her disapproving conscience.

"What the hell is the matter with you?" Issa heard Ishaan's voice to her left. He was holding Gigi's arm, both looking horrified. "Rake is telling the whole school you guys slept together and you don't even care?"

A lie. It was a lie. Ishaan couldn't stand not being the number-one guy in her life anymore. He was spreading these horrible lies.

"How could you do that to someone who lives with you!" Gigi's expression was of disgust.

Even they were turning on her now. First Alisha, now her so-called friends? Ishaan spreading rumors about her to the whole school with Gigi by his side.

Issa sneered. "Listen to yourself, guys. This is Cat Morena we're talking about. The girl who two months ago stole my boyfriend and humiliated me in front of the whole school. Remember? You guys were there!"

"Cat is no saint," Ishaan started. "But—"

"But, Iz, this isn't you! You're acting so horrible…

much worse than Cat! And hanging out with those Belles all the time?"

"Those girls are so stupid and shallow. And you're beginning to look and sound like them every day!" Ishaan raised his voice at her for probably the first time since they'd known each other.

What was this, an intervention? How dare her friends gang up on her like that?

"Oh, oh!" Issa took a step back and realized they had backed her into the door. "I'm shallow? Uh, Gigi, weren't you the one who made me buy these clothes? Weren't you the one who told me I should go for it if I liked a guy? Who said I needed to get over Adam?"

"Iz, I wanted you to be confident about yourself, not start acting like a major bitch!" Gigi snapped.

Issa felt like someone had slapped her. Her cheeks burned. Gigi was calling her a bitch in public. Ishaan was spreading rumors of her night with Rake around school and then blaming him. These people were supposed to be her best friends?

"Okay, I get it!" Issa replaced the scowl on her face with a serene smile, Belle-style. "You're jealous. You're jealous I'm popular, every guy wants to get with me and you can't even get Ishaan. I get it, Gigi!"

Gigi's eyes filled with tears but Issa felt not a drop of remorse. Gigi had asked for it.

"If you can treat your future sister like crap, I don't know why you would treat me any better," Gigi whispered.

Issa stood alone in the hallway as the bell rang, watching Ishaan and Gigi turn their backs on her and walk away.

CHAPTER 15

Insanity Is Hereditary: You Get it From Your Children

Issa looked out of the window of the guest house when she heard a car engine pull in, hoping it was Rake or one of the Belles. She'd been frantically catching up on her extra-credit assignment and readings. She'd been a total hermit for the past three days and was ready for some company.

Alisha and Cat got out of the sparkling Bentley, both laughing and talking. Issa glanced at the time. Almost 7:00 p.m.—too late for them to just be getting back from school. Where had they been on a Thursday night? And why were they laughing as if they shared an amazing joke.

Issa felt a twinge. Alisha used to only laugh like that with her once upon a time.

Cat lugged a package out of the backseat and said something to Alisha. A brown-paper-wrapped package.

"It's yours," Issa heard Alisha yell.

Issa felt like she was going to explode. She could feel her

ears heating up. First her mother grounded her, then took Cat out and bought her presents. This had to be revenge for not telling her about Rake.

Issa was glowering by the time Alisha finally tore herself away from Cat and made it inside the guest house.

"Where have you been?" she demanded the second Alisha kicked off her beige cowboy boots and flopped onto a kitchen stool.

"Nice to see you too. How's the studying going? Are you out of community-college territory yet?" Despite their silence over the past few days, Alisha sounded like she was in a great mood tonight.

Issa made a face. Community college. She'd shoot herself first. "Wonderful. Where have you been?"

"At the art show."

"What art show?"

"The one in New Haven."

Issa frowned. She and Alisha always went to art shows together. Alisha always wanted to buy expensive abstract originals and Issa always restrained her. It was their thing. Even though they hadn't been superclose lately, Issa couldn't believe Alisha had gone without her. And had dared to take Cat instead.

"Did you have fun without me?" The bitterness in her voice wasn't lost on Alisha.

"I asked you if you wanted to go last week, but you said you had better things to do." Alisha hoisted herself off the stool and started puttering around in the refrigerator.

"So you went with Cat."

"Yup." Alisha poured mango-lime juice into a glass.

"She's in my oils class, remember? She's doing really well and I thought she would like to see the show."

Issa didn't respond. Cat Morena doing well in one of the hardest classes at the school. Huh. She had to be up to something. Issa doubted Cat had developed a sudden interest in greasy paint and sketch pads. In fact, Issa had a very good feeling Cat was poisoning Alisha's mind. Maybe a few subtle suggestions placed into Alisha's head had led to Issa's grounding.

"Are you done with all your homework?" Alisha asked. "It's about dinnertime."

The last thing Issa could think about now was the policies in the Middle East.

"I'm just surprised Cat wanted to go." Issa closed her World Politics textbook. "I mean, all she cares about are clothes and boys."

"Actually, that seems more like you nowadays. Cat's really surprising me." Alisha set her empty glass in the kitchen sink. "I'll see you at the house for dinner."

Issa stared at the empty glass, still smarting from Alisha's last comment. Her mother had changed so much. Putting away dishes, driving a Bentley, marrying someone she knew Issa couldn't stand.

Issa lowered herself back into the chair. Everything was changing.

Alisha had made good on her promise and removed both Cat's and Issa's names from the Snow Queen ballots. The only name that would be present would be Jenni Wilson.

The Belles had been furious and vowed to get Issa's name

back on at the last minute and use their influence to make sure she won.

Issa knew Serena would be able to pull it off, but it wouldn't do her any good if she was still grounded. The Snow Ball committee would call out her name at the dance and ask her to collect her crown while she sat in her bedroom doing calculus homework.

That would never do.

Issa remained silent at dinner. She kept an eye on Cat, who was smiling and talking to Alisha and Diego about the art show and the painting Alisha had bought her.

"Sounds like my girls had a great evening." Diego couldn't take his eyes off Alisha in an off-the-shoulder burgundy sweater dress, her wavy hair swept up in a loose chignon.

"We really did. Cat learned quite a bit in art history last year apparently. She knew all about modernism versus cubism—"

"Oh, but I had no idea how to tell if something was original versus a copy. They had paintings there, originals right next to fakes. Alisha showed me how to tell them apart. It was all about the signatures."

Issa tuned out. Being locked up at home was making Cat an outrageously good actress. Issa almost started to believe that Cat had had a good time.

Issa swirled her water glass around, watching the ice cubes clink together. She needed to figure out a way to get out of her so-called grounding. Alisha had never grounded her in her life. It had to be something she'd picked up from Diego. Issa knew her mother and knew how much Alisha had hated all the rules and restrictions her own parents had placed on her.

The Snow Ball was next weekend, three days after the English final. Doing well on the final alone wouldn't get Alisha off her back. An idea started to form in Issa's head. It had the potential to end in disaster, but it was a risk worth taking. It was her only choice.

"Hey, guys."

All three looked toward her.

"I was thinking. Cat and I have an English final next week and I don't know about her..." Issa did her best to give Cat an earnest look "...but I am *so* not ready."

Alisha and Diego glanced at each other, Alisha looking confused, Diego disturbed.

"I thought maybe if Cat and I studied together, like non-stop for the next week, and we both did well..."

Cat shot Issa a look that practically screamed, "What the hell are you doing?"

"What I was thinking is that if we both do well on the final, we should be able to go to the Snow Ball. Both of us."

Issa heard Cat suck in her breath.

"Well." Diego set his napkin on the table. "I think that's a fine idea. But Alisha has to agree."

Alisha stared hard at Issa.

Issa squirmed. Her mother knew her better than anyone. She was totally going to see through this little scheme. And then she was dead.

A slow smile formed on Alisha's face. "I think that's the best idea I've heard all day."

Or maybe not.

Issa let out a sigh of relief.

"I'll even up the stakes. I'll make sure Professor Kidlinger grades both of your exams next Thursday morning. If you both get As, I will personally take the day off on Friday. I want to take both of you into the city to buy whatever dresses you want for the dance. DKNY, Carolina, whatever you want."

Cat practically shrieked with excitement. Even Issa smiled. Her emerald-green vision of a Prada gown was going to come true. She could feel it.

"That sounds great, Mom. We can do this, can't we, Cat?"

"Yeah, we can!" Cat turned to Issa with a toothy grin.

Issa held Cat's gaze. For that one instant, Issa saw her own excitement reflected in Cat's eyes. She could swear Cat was smiling at her for real.

Issa wanted the glow of the moment to last, but instead felt nauseated thinking of why she wanted to go to the dance so badly. So she could flounce in with Rake on her arm, collect the Snow Queen crown and humiliate Cat in front of the whole school.

Maybe this wasn't such a good idea. As much as she hated to admit it, she liked this moment the four of them were sharing. They were almost a family. A dysfunctional, overly materialistic family, but a family nonetheless. Alisha looked so happy zooming around town in the Bentley. And Issa could practically feel the satin of the Prada gown against her skin. Maybe…

"Also, another bit of news," Diego broke in. "Alisha and I will be looking at wedding sites outside the city next weekend. Make sure you girls stay out of trouble. No throwing any post-dance parties."

Wedding sites. Alisha was marrying Diego in a month. Roy would disappear for good and Issa knew she would never see him again.

Issa's happy haze crumbled around her and she again saw her situation in stark gray and white.

Her mother could *not* marry Diego. Ever.

After Issa was crowned Snow Queen and Cat had a nervous breakdown, there was no doubt that the wedding would be called off.

CHAPTER 16

The Road to Success Is Always Under Construction

"**Listen** up. This is important."

Issa was rudely awakened on Saturday morning by a sun-drenched figure standing over her.

"Who?" Issa reached up to shield her eyes from the flood of sunshine in her room. She'd gotten to bed well past midnight last night after a serious calculus session intermingled with secret phone calls to Rake. "What are you doing in my room?"

"We need to study for that English test." Cat was tapping her foot, holding a stack of books. "I'm sick of my room. I thought we could do it here."

Issa had overlooked one thing in her quest to get off grounding. She would actually have to spend time with Cat.

"It's freaking early," Issa mumbled, and burrowed deeper into the comforter.

"Look, I didn't pay attention the first three months of

class. I have no idea what we covered. I know you got As that whole time and I need your help."

Issa opened one eye. Cat was being honest and admitting she needed help. *Twilight Zone*. Was she dreaming?

Another shake and the warm down comforter being pulled off her assured her this was no dream.

"All right, all right. Give me, like, an hour. I need to get ready."

Cat rolled her eyes. "Ten minutes. I'll put the coffee on."

Twenty minutes later, Issa strolled into the kitchen hoping Cat had gotten bored and left. But no, she was sitting at the kitchen table, stack of books spread out, her half-pound Sony Vaio laptop in front of her, half-finished cup of coffee in her hand.

"Nice outfit. Your coffee's over there."

Issa glanced down at her outfit. Was that a real compliment? It *was* a nice outfit. Cashmere fitted hoodie, denim mini and black furry platform boots.

"I have the same shoes," Cat commented as Issa took a seat, coffee in hand. "So comfy, right?"

"Uh, so where do you want to start?" Issa didn't know what to make of Cat's new attitude toward her. She wasn't even going to try to figure it out so early in the morning.

"Well, here's the syllabus. And I brought all the books. Plus the Cliff's Notes. Why don't we go through and discuss each reading? I'll take notes and print us each a copy when we're done."

Issa actually thought that was a pretty good plan. And was surprised Cat had come up with it. "Sure. Okay. Um, the first reading was—"

"*Pride and Prejudice.*" Cat held up a copy of the book. "Let's make sure we know all the study-guide questions. Who was Pride and who was Prejudice?"

Issa started to give her standard answer of Elizabeth being prejudiced against Mr. Darcy's wealth, but Cat cut her off. "See, I think Mr. Darcy has too much pride and Lizzie—"

"Hold on." Issa held up her hand. "I thought you hadn't done any of the readings."

"Duh." Cat rolled her eyes. "The book is freaking long. I saw the movie with Kiera Knightly and that hot English guy."

Figured. The only thing Cat looked like she'd ever read was *Cosmo Girl*. But still, Issa was a tiny bit impressed Cat had an opinion on *Pride and Prejudice*.

"What did you think of Mr. Bingley?" Issa asked.

"Total loser." Cat giggled.

Issa almost laughed too. First time she'd heard anyone refer to a literary figure as a "total loser."

Cat continued talking. "I mean, if he loved Jane, why the hell did he listen to that snooty sister anyway? I mean, if he's going to follow the crowd all the time…then…"

Cat stopped talking and looked away. Issa could feel the tips of her ears flaming. Both she and Cat were guilty of following the crowd and Cat seemed aware of it.

"Yeah, good thing everything worked out in the end, right?" asked Issa softly, touching the worn cover of the book in front of her.

"Definitely. I think things usually work out in the end. Maybe not like the main characters wanted, but definitely for the best."

Issa swallowed. Everything worked out in stories, true.

"You know," Cat said after a brief silence, "I'm pretty glad neither you nor I are doing the whole Snow Queen thing. It's not really that great. You win one of these, and then people expect you to win all of them."

Issa smiled weakly. "Right, it's pretty silly. I don't know what I was thinking."

Cat was going to be doomed as a social outcast once Issa won the Snow Queen crown. The Belles would make sure of that.

Issa took another sip of coffee to squash the queasy feeling in her stomach. "Okay, let's get back to this. What was the next book?"

Cat passed her a copy of *To The Lighthouse*.

The morning of the English final rolled around too soon. Issa watched Ishaan as he came in and took a seat. He seemed to have chosen the farthest possible desk from her. Neither he nor Gigi had called her even once to apologize. She took a swig of her coconut latte. This was not the time to get thinking about them.

"God, I am so friggin' tired." Cat arrived and set down her venti mocha on the edge of her desk. "Damn, don't tell *Papi* I used the Lord's name in vain."

Issa laughed. Cat could be really funny when she tried. "I think we're ready."

Issa and Cat had studied nonstop for the exam for the past week. Cat had gotten a major case of the nerves the previous night and Issa had assured her everything would work out fine.

Alisha had been eavesdropping on them and pretending not to. Issa had laid it on really thick.

"You're going to do so well. And we're going to New York City to get these amazing gowns!"

Cat had smiled weakly. "I'm going to hurl."

This morning she wasn't nearly as green, but still looked nervous. "I'll be so glad when this is over."

"Make that two," Issa muttered, but she didn't completely mean it. She hadn't understood what had been happening over the past few days. She and Cat had been perfectly civil to each other, skillfully avoiding controversial topics. Cat hadn't brought up Adam even once and Issa made it a point to not mention the Snow Ball. It was almost as if she and Cat were...friends?

Not possible. Cat would go back to hating her in a few hours.

"Good luck," Issa couldn't help but whisper to Cat as Professor Kidlinger started passing out the exams.

"You too."

As Ishaan turned to pass the stack of exams to the person behind him, he locked eyes with Issa. He looked confused when he saw her talking to Cat.

Issa looked away. No distractions. Her Prada gown and Snow Queen crown were calling her.

"I don't believe it. I still don't believe it!" Cat's excitement was practically spilling out of her as she, Alisha and Issa perused Bergdorf Goodman on Friday.

"Both of you. Perfect scores. I don't know how you did it. Except for massive cheating, huh?"

Issa shook her head. In her wildest dreams, she hadn't imagined *both* she and Cat would ace that final. Professor Kidlinger had personally come up and congratulated her and told her how proud she was. Then she'd done the same with Cat, but Issa had felt no jealousy. Cat had deserved it. She had organized all the study sessions and she had gone without sleep for four days for that prize.

"I'm so proud of my girls." Alisha was smiling as she held up a red velvet Guenivere-esque dress.

Issa's smiled faded. *Her girls?*

"I like that!" Cat pointed at Alisha's gown. "Are you going to wear something like that for the wedding?"

"You know, I hadn't thought about it."

"Oh my God, we totally have to go to the Vera Wang store. She makes the *best* wedding dresses. Right, Issa?"

Issa's mood continued to darken. Vera Wang? Wedding? Not if she had anything to say about it.

"Sure," she answered shortly, and gestured toward another rack. "I'm going to look at the Pradas."

Alisha and Cat barely seemed to hear her as they continued to chatter about the wedding. Issa, feeling left out and sad, barely registered the pile of dresses she collected in her arms.

Half an hour later, she had tried on every Prada gown. She didn't like a single one. This day was not turning out like she'd expected. She'd imagined an exciting trip to the city like she and Alisha used to make. Laughing and giggling. Having fabulous desserts for lunch. Buying cute shoes from independent boutiques.

Instead Alisha and Cat had been practically joined at the

hip. Like mother and daughter. They seemed to like the same clothes and kept finding things they had in common. Like they both thought *Gigi* was the best movie ever. Issa had argued that if there was a best movie ever, it was once and for all *Legends of the Fall*. They had both laughed and said Brad Pitt was no match for Maurice Chevalier.

Issa sighed and ventured out of the dressing room. This shopping trip was looking to be a bust. She hadn't found anything close to the dress she'd been looking for. Everything she'd picked up was drab, boring and ugh.

Cat poked her head out of the dressing room. "What do you think of this? It's Ellie Tahari."

She stepped out and twirled.

Issa gasped. It was the dress from her visions. The emerald-green satin gown with shirred off-the-shoulder straps. Cat's creamy skin practically seemed to glow against the dress.

"It's gorgeous!" Alisha said from behind Issa. "It's perfect. Doesn't she look amazing?"

Issa had to admit Cat did look great. Her tiny, size-2 body held the Tahari dress perfectly. But it wasn't a dress for Cat. It was a dress for Issa. It was a dress for a Snow Queen.

"Yeah, it's pretty perfect," Issa muttered. She was ready to leave. This trip should have been made with the Belles, not Alisha and Cat. But it was too late now. Cat had her dream dress and Issa knew she wouldn't find anything better. Maybe she would find something else in New Joliet.

Cat caught Issa's eye in the mirror as Issa gazed jealously at the dress. "Actually, I don't think it's my size. Iz, why don't you try it on? I have a feeling this will look amazing against your skin."

"But—" Before Issa could protest further, Cat had ducked back into the dressing room. Within seconds the dress was in Issa's arms.

Issa hesitated for a second. Did she really want Cat's pity or sympathy or whatever it was? Curiosity got the best of her. She slipped into the dressing room and slid into the dress.

The shimmery green material floated around her in a haze. She'd undergone a transformation. Her skin glowed, her hair fell just right over her shoulders, the mermaid hem of the gown highlighted her curvy figure perfectly.

The gown had made her into a star.

She shyly opened the dressing room door. "I think it's too tight."

Cat's and Alisha's expressions assured her it wasn't true.

"That's it. That's the dress for you." Cat pointed at her. "You're getting it. My dad would insist."

"But—"

"Say thanks to Cat," Alisha prodded.

"I—but, you sure?"

Issa was afraid of the game Cat was playing. Why was she being so nice?

"Of course!" Cat smiled in response. "I saw this great white one that I think would work for me. Iz, do you want to see it?"

Issa felt like she was suffocating in her guilt. Why, oh, why was Cat being like this? Why was she treating Issa like family now? It had to be just an act to get on Alisha's good side. There was no other explanation. "Sure, let me get out of this."

Issa felt guilty tears trying to squeeze themselves out of her eyes and she hung the dress back on the silk-covered hanger.

"Figures, huh?" Cat twirled in an ivory gown with a tulle skirt. "Look at us. Two major babes in totally hot dresses. And neither of us is going to be the Snow Queen. It'll go to that Jenni chick who's never worn a dress in her life."

Issa looked anywhere but at Cat. "Right, neither of us. Major babes. What a shame," she mumbled.

"Maybe next year." Alisha smiled and lay a hand on Issa's shoulder.

Issa smiled weakly at her.

"I am so proud of you," Alisha whispered, and kissed Issa on the side of the head. "Now that you babes have your dresses…gelato time!"

Just one more day. One more day and all this would be over.

Suddenly she found herself wishing the Snow Ball would never happen. A lot of people were going to be hurt: Cat, Diego and most of all Alisha. And it would be all her fault.

There was still time. She could call Serena and have the ballot reverted. It was the only way. Cat was being too nice for Issa to pull such a horrible trick.

Issa slowed down her steps and let Alisha and Cat go ahead of her into Gelatiamo. She had to call Serena.

She was about to use her cell phone when Cat reached over and strung her arm through Alisha's.

Issa frowned. She still wasn't used to the sudden closeness of her mother and her archenemy. But she could get used to sharing Alisha. After all, Cat had had to share Diego.

Issa heard Cat whisper to Alisha, "I can't wait till Adam comes over and we take pictures together before the dance. I'm pretty sure this is going to be, like, the best night ever."

Alisha smiled and squeezed Cat's arm. "He's a nice kid."

"I really like him."

Fury streaked though Issa and she released her grip on her phone. Of course Cat hadn't changed. This was just an act in front of Alisha. The first chance Cat got she would revert to her standard spoiled-bitch attitude and flaunt Issa's ex-boyfriend in front of her.

But what if Cat really likes Adam? Like actually likes him? Issa's tiny conscience whispered.

Not possible. Issa started to shake with anger. Cat's one and only goal in life was to make Issa look bad.

The plan was still on. Cat was going down.

CHAPTER 17

It Matters Not Whether You Win or Lose; What Matters Is Whether I Win or Lose

"**One** more picture of my girls." Diego held up his fancy camera again. "Come stand in the front hallway."

Issa gritted her teeth. Why was he doing this? All she wanted was to go to the ball and get this whole night over with.

"Smile!" Diego called.

Issa forced a fake grin and even placed an arm around Cat as they posed in front of the French doors. Cat hesitantly placed an arm around Issa, as well.

Cat's Chanel No 22 perfume infiltrated Issa's senses as Diego took the picture. She knew how the picture would turn out. Two pretty brunette high-school girls, one in a white gown, one in green. Both smiling, looking like they had no cares in the world. Looking happy. Looking like they liked each other. Like they were sisters.

After this weekend, Diego would burn all the pictures

from tonight and definitely ask Issa and Alisha to leave. They would go back to Roy's—their house in the D.

Issa tried to cheer up at the thought of being with her father again, but all she felt was dread thinking of the moment she would be crowned Snow Queen. Alisha would be furious that she'd sneakily gotten her name on the ballot again. And Diego? He would just be disappointed in her and would listen to Cat when she begged her father to not marry Alisha. Cat would come out looking like the good guy in all of this and Issa would be the underhanded psycho who was out to destroy a potential family.

For you, Dad.

"There we go. What beautiful girls. Now, we had really better be leaving." Diego replaced his camera in its case. "We'll lose our reservation at the bed-and-breakfast unless we're there in the next hour or so."

Issa grimaced. Her mother and Diego. In a romantic B&B in Hartford. Spending the night together. Waking up late the next morning, looking at locations to have their wedding ceremony in. The thought made her sick.

"I'm here. I'm here." Alisha ran out of the kitchen dragging a Louis Vuitton carry-on behind her. A real Louis Vuitton. A thank-you gift from Cat. "Okay, both of you girls have rides to the dance, yes?"

Issa nodded.

Cat bit her lip. "I was just going to drive myself?"

"Oh." Alisha stopped. "What happened to—" She glanced at Issa and stopped.

"Adam?" Issa supplied. Where had all of Cat's big plans of flaunting Adam during the "best night of his life" gone?

"He'll meet me there," Cat said nonchalantly. "I'll drive myself."

Issa's curiosity was piqued. Cat wasn't going to make her grand entrance at the dance with a date on her arm? What was going on here?

"All right. You have our cell numbers. Call if you need anything. I've left a list of places we'll be visiting on the refrigerator." Diego appeared to be paying no attention to his daughter's latest romantic development. "*Tenga cuidado,* both of you. Be careful. Don't open the door to strangers."

Cat laughed. "*Papi,* we're not *ninos.* Please!"

"Let's go, babe." Alisha lay a hand on Diego's arm. "Take care, girls. Love you!" she called as they sailed out the door.

Cat and Issa stared at each other after the door had closed.

The nice-girl act could stop now. The parents were gone. Cat could show her claws again.

Issa braced herself.

"You really do look great. Are you, um, going with Rake?"

Issa nodded. Here it came.

"That's good. He seems cool. Kinda quiet, though."

Issa had no idea what to say. When was Cat going to turn back into Cat?

"Um, yeah." Issa cleared her throat. "Well, I'm going to go to the guest house and call some people to make sure they're ready."

"Okay." Cat just stood at the base of the stairs, looking lost. Issa realized Cat no longer had anyone to call. Jewel and Sunshine were now hanging around with the senior cheerleader crowd. Cat was out.

"I'll see you at the dance." Issa forced herself to sound cheerful.

"Bye." Cat was still standing on the stairs when Issa closed the door behind her.

"Ohmygod, you look so great!" Megan Simmons ran up to Issa and Rake as they entered the ballroom at the Westin Hotel. "Ohmygod, the Belles are totally going to want to get a picture together. You totally have to come with me."

Rake squeezed her arm and whispered into her hair, "How long do we have to be with those chicks? She is so freaking loud."

"Not long, babe," Issa whispered before smiling at Megan. "Wow! I love that color on you! You look totally like Kate Moss. But without the whole cocaine thing."

Megan glowed, looking nothing like Kate Moss, her already tanned cheeks reddening. "Come on! Serena's totally waiting."

"I'm going to get drinks for us." Rake winked at Issa and strolled to where a group of guys, all the Belles' dates plus a few jocks, were standing around the punch bowl trying to look innocent. Issa had a feeling someone was going to spike the punch with a hidden flask in the next half hour.

"I told the girls about my mom," Megan whispered as the girls headed toward the Belles. "And they thought it was so cool. I'm half Caribbean! It's only, like, the best vacation spot in the world! We're all going to go over spring break so I can understand my heritage and stuff. You should totally come!"

Issa smiled. Leave it to Megan to turn a revelation about her mother into a fun-in-the-sun adventure.

"So, tonight's the night," Serena said as she hugged Issa with the standard Belle hug, cheeks touching with barely any body contact. "Your first time onstage as Athens High royalty. Excited?"

"Yeah," Issa said, trying not to let the waltzing butterflies in her stomach become apparent.

"Where's Cat?" Serena searched the crowd of people. "I haven't seen her or that pathetic Adam kid all night."

Issa turned to look. Serena was right. Cat was nowhere to be seen. She, however, did notice Gigi entering the ballroom, in a gorgeous strapless pink number. She was more surprised by the guy with his arm through Gigi's. Ishaan. He leaned down and whispered something in her ear and she laughed.

Well, they seemed to have moved on quickly. Issa tried to calm the jealousy streaking through her. Why did she care anyway? She was about to get everything she'd ever wanted. Let them have each other and spend the rest of their lives talking about how much they hated her.

Even as she turned away from Gigi and Ishaan, she could almost feel the silkiness of Ishaan's faint stubble against her cheek. She could feel her cheeks heating up. She was thinking stupid thoughts. She was here with a gorgeous guy who was obviously crazy about her. What did she want with overly critical Ishaan anyway?

"Drink up." A plastic wineglass filled to the brim with a suspicious liquid appeared from behind her. A moment later, she felt Rake's lips on the back of her neck.

She accepted the glass and turned to find herself folded into Rake's arms. "Let's get this crown of yours and get out of here," he whispered in her ear. "Your parents are out of town, right? Let's go back to your place. We can finish what we started the other night." He traced a finger down her back.

Issa felt chills run down her spine. The other night. She could barely remember what they had started, and her grounding had given her a good excuse to stay away from any other close encounters of the Rake kind. She wasn't quite sure if she was ready for the next step that he was obviously expecting.

"Oooh, he is so hot!" Megan whispered to Issa as soon as Rake turned around to talk to Megan's date. "What did he just ask you? To go back to your place? Wow! Hot!"

Issa managed a smile. "Yeah. I guess."

"You're on the pill and stuff, right?"

Issa didn't answer. The pill? Yeah, right. Alisha would have her head on a platter.

"All of us got on it as soon as we turned fourteen. What about you? It's *so* important, right?"

"Yeah, me too. The pill. Yay." Suddenly, Issa wanted nothing more than to get out of there. "I need to get some air."

She whispered an excuse about the ladies' room to Rake and made her way out to the balcony. She leaned against the railing and pressed the cold glass against her cheeks.

What had she gotten herself into? The so-called cool crowd seemed to be way over her head. Apparently all of the Belles had been having sex since fourteen. Rake expected that she would sleep with him after they'd been together for only a month. She didn't know how to tell him she was a virgin and really, she wanted to wait awhile.

She took a deep breath. She was overreacting. She would

explain to Rake that she wasn't ready. A fuzzy memory of Rake's hand inside her dress even after she'd asked him to stop came back to her. He had to listen to her tonight. She would stay completely sober this time.

"Hey, Iz." She whirled around at the voice.

Adam.

He stood ten feet away, wearing a tuxedo, his dirty blond hair spiked up in front. Glasses gone. Acne greatly reduced.

She barely recognized him. Cat had performed some sort of miraculous makeover on him.

"Adam. Hey. What's going on?"

"I need to talk to you." He was suddenly standing very close to her. "Listen, I—I still love you. And I'm so sorry."

What the hell was he saying? Was he already drunk from the potent punch?

"Where's Cat?" Issa took a step back. He was too close. She never thought she would feel uncomfortable having Adam so close to her. This was Adam. She'd known him since before he'd even had facial hair. But knowing he was Cat's boyfriend and if she came out here at that moment…

Adam reached out and grabbed her arm. "I broke up with her."

"You what!"

Issa couldn't fake a cool exterior. Adam had broken up with her for Cat. Then he broke up with Cat for her. He had to be insane or something.

"Look, Adam. I don't think—"

"No, no, please hear me out. Please. We are so good together. I was such an idiot. I mean, I forgot how much you meant to me."

Some of the emotions from the day he'd broken up with her started to flood back. "You forgot how much I meant to you when? When Cat got you into her hot tub? You lost your memory at that second?"

"You know what she's like! I mean, I was caught up in the moment and—I just want you back so badly."

Issa pushed him away. So this was why Cat had come to the dance alone. She couldn't help but feel sorry for Cat. Once the most popular girl in school, she was now dumped by Adam Mitchell before the Snow Ball. Everyone would know by tomorrow morning.

"I'm sorry, Adam, but honestly, I haven't thought about you in months. I think maybe it's time you took a break from girlfriends."

With that she pushed him away. One last glance back at this stricken face told her that hadn't been the answer he'd been expecting. Too bad.

So strange. When he'd broken up with her, she'd imagined that same scene in her head a hundred times. Never had it ended the way it just did. She just didn't want to be with him anymore. She'd never realized it before, but Adam was kind of a loser. What the hell had she been thinking?

Sheeeeeeeeeeeee.

Issa jumped at the sound of microphone feedback.

The chairperson of the dance committee tapped the microphone, earning shrieks from the crowd. "Ladies. Gentlemen. Please give your attention to me. Up here on the stage. No, not down your date's dress. Here."

"There you are!" Megan appeared from nowhere and grabbed her arm. "We've been looking for you everywhere."

But Issa wasn't seeing Megan. Her eyes were on Cat. She was sitting in the back of the room in the corner, head held in her hands, her shoulders shaking. She didn't seem to be taking the breakup with Adam well.

Suddenly, she wanted to go to Cat. Just sit next to her and tell her Adam was so not worth it. She took a step toward Cat, but Megan firmly pulled her in the other direction.

The announcer continued. "Let's all raise our glasses to this year's Snow Queen."

Issa found herself standing next to Rake a few steps away from the stage.

No, no. Not now. Not like this.

"Our Snow Queen. Isabelle Mazumder!"

The spotlight fell on Issa and Rake. The student body burst into applause and Issa was ushered onto the stage. The bright lights shone in her eyes as a heavy silver tiara was placed on her head. It felt like a crushing helmet. She raised her hand to block out the light in her eyes. She couldn't see anything. Not even the audience.

"Now the Snow Queen will choose a King to have her first dance with."

Before Issa could say a word, Rake appeared onstage a second later. Applause boomed from the audience as Rake pulled Issa into his arms and kissed her.

She pulled away and tried to shove the tiara out of her eyes.

This was not how it was supposed to be. She was supposed to be triumphant. This was her moment. The moment she'd been waiting for two months for. Instead, she just felt dread and disappointment in herself. She had played dirty and it had worked. She'd gotten what she'd wanted so badly. Rake, the spotlight, Cat crying in the back of the room. But she'd never felt so low.

Issa dared to glance into the crowd as Rake led her to the dance floor.

Cat hadn't moved. One hand was over her mouth and her eyes were locked on Issa's. A few feet away, Gigi and Ishaan stood, holding hands, both looking disappointed. The three of them were the only people in the room not applauding.

CHAPTER 18

The Nice Thing About Being a Celebrity Is That If You Bore People They Think It's Their Fault

"This place is awesome! Who's bringing the music?" Rake's soccer teammate Ralphie ran through the front doors of the Morena mansion, six-pack of beer in his right hand, cell phone in his left.

Issa tailed close behind to make sure the soccer team didn't do too much damage on their way out to the deck. Looked like Ralphie was spreading the news of the party to beyond just the soccer team and the cheerleaders.

"Damn these idiots," Rake grumbled as he followed Issa. "Whose idea was this party anyway?"

Issa shrugged innocently. "One of the guys, I guess. Cat must have said it was fine with her."

The lies just kept on building. She couldn't remember the last person she'd been honest with lately.

I had no choice, she told herself. *This lie was totally justified.*

After their first dance as Snow Queen and King, Rake was practically pulling her off the dance floor in his eagerness to get her to leave…and out of her gown.

Issa had sweetly excused herself and asked Megan to spread the word that there was a happening post-party party at the Morena mansion. As predicted, half the school was now parking their cars on the vast driveway and on the street. Rake's disposition was darkening more and more by the second.

"If I wanted to come to one of these stupid parties, I would have done it when Cat Morena was throwing them every weekend," he grumbled. "Why don't you and I go out back for a bit and leave these clowns alone?"

"Um, well—"

"You said you wanted to be alone with me, right? I hear the hot tub's pretty private."

Issa hoped and prayed it wasn't *too* private. She would have to take her chances. "I'll go change."

"Leave your crown on. It's hot."

Bathing suit and a crown sounded a bit too Miss America for her. All she needed was a speech about saving the world from bad hairdos and she was all set.

Issa shivered as she ran back to the guest house. She couldn't believe she was throwing a wild, Cat Morena–style party. At the dance, she had felt like she was on a high. Everyone coming up to her, telling her how beautiful she was, how hot she and Rake were. The night had been unbelievable so far, despite the nagging guilt that weighed her down more than the ten pounds of bling she wore around her neck.

Cat had quietly disappeared from the ballroom sometime

during the night. Issa hadn't seen her, Gigi or Ishaan since. She had, however, seen Adam. He stood in the shadows and didn't take his eyes off her once. She put those thoughts out of her head and tried to focus on the present.

She stared at herself in the mirror after taking off her formal jewelry and putting on her brand-new bikini. Per Rake's request, she left the tiara on her head. She'd never shown so much skin before. She was wondering if this was such a good idea considering Rake's amorous mood that night.

Before she could deliberate further, she heard the thumping sound of loud 50 Cent music as another round of cars pulled into the driveway. She sighed and ran out to see what was happening.

What the hell... Issa stood out on the driveway, a cover-up tightly wrapped around her waist. The whole school seemed to have shown up. Girls still in their formal gowns and guys in half-undone tuxedos were storming the house.

Issa shook her head as she ran for the house. Word did travel fast. She did a quick check around the living room and deck. Everyone was just flirting and drinking beer. Nothing broken, no fiascos. Looked like her first crazy party was going to be a success.

"There you are." Rake's voice in her ear startled her. "Come on. Let's go out. I want to see this infamous hot tub."

Issa took one more look around the house. The Belles were laughing with their dates in the corner. Serena raised a filled champagne glass in Issa's direction. Issa wiggled her fingers in response. She wanted to stay here and enjoy her party, but Rake was tugging insistently at her hand.

She would spend fifteen minutes in the tub with him, kiss

him a bunch of times and get back to the fun. Then if Rake left, he left. She would make this up to him later.

Issa led Rake through the expansive garden to the gazebo. The lights from the house suddenly seemed far away as she stripped off her cover-up and hopped quickly into the tub.

Rake watched in amusement as she sat on the lowest step so she was neck deep in the streaming water. He didn't seem even slightly embarrassed as he shucked off his formal wear and slid into the water in only his boxers. His tentlike boxers.

Issa circled the tub, keeping a distance between them.

Rake grinned. "Aren't you a tease?"

Issa forced a laugh.

"Come here." Before she could move, he was next to her. He leaned in and kissed her, running his hands through her damp hair.

That was nice. She wished it could just stay this way. She saw nothing wrong with just prolonging those amazing, knee-weakening kisses.

He grazed her cheeks with his fingers and deepened his kiss. Very nice.

He slid his hands down over her shoulders, still kissing her.

He was so strong and solid. And smelled so good. She wrapped her arms around his neck and pulled him in closer.

"Baby," he groaned.

She practically purred. "Yes?"

Suddenly she felt water swirling in places it hadn't been a second before and her bikini top floated to the surface.

He'd untied her top.

Issa gasped. "What's wrong with you?"

She grabbed her top and slid down as far as she could and retied her bikini with a double knot.

"Oh, come on." Rake made another move toward her. "How long are we going to play this game?"

Issa stood up too. "Look, I know what you want. But honestly, we've just been dating, like, a month. I'm not ready."

"Well, you've been acting ready since we met. You practically gave me a strip show on the soccer field. What was that all about?"

Issa opened her mouth. "I was just—flirting with you."

Rake took a step toward her. "Guess what, baby. Taking off your clothes when meeting a guy for the first time says something about a girl."

"I'm not that kind of girl." Issa backed away. "I think you should leave."

"Actually." Rake stood up, water streaming down his muscular chest as he tossed a towel in her direction. "You are. Throwing yourself at me, wearing skirts so short they could be headbands, inviting me into your hot tub. You're *exactly* that kind of girl. And everyone at school knows it."

Issa watched him leave, not even the least bit sorry.

CHAPTER 19

Don't Regret Doing Things, Regret Getting Caught

who were these people? These weren't juniors or seniors from her school who were doing shots off a girl's bare belly on the floor of the living room. They looked older, much older.

There was a suspicious greenish puke-colored stain on the carpet under the girl.

Damn.

Issa ran through the house to see who else was around to help her. The Belles seemed to have cleared out. A few members of the soccer team were standing around the dining-room table, playing vodka roulette on the lazy Susan. Issa had never been so happy to see a bunch of drunk jocks. At least they were familiar drunk jocks.

"Guys! Who are those people in the living room? And who is that half-naked girl?"

Ralphie, glazy-eyed, turned to her. "Wow, you're pretty

hot in that bikini. Wanna get into the hot tub with me? Rake said he was done with you."

Done with her? As if she was a used tracksuit. Issa fumed. "Go to hell."

"Oooh, I likey!" Ralphie yelled. "Rake said you were a feisty one!"

She heard the sound of a crash and glass shattering as she ran from the room. "Keep dreaming, you little freak!"

What had she ever seen in Rake? Obviously it had been him who'd spread those vicious lies about her. Now the whole school thought she was a slut.

"Agrh." Issa ran back into the living room. The hideous shot game had progressed to each guy taking a bite of lime that was in the mystery girl's mouth.

Gross.

"All right. Everybody. Let's clear out of here," she yelled as loudly as she could.

Nobody listened. The girl sat up and grabbed the nearest guy and started making out with him to the delight of the rest of the guys. They whooped and cheered.

Issa cringed. Was that the kind of girl she had been on track to becoming?

"What the hell is going on here?"

Issa whirled around to see Cat, still in her lace gown. Her face seemed to be cleared of all makeup and her hair was up in a ponytail. Issa had never in her life been so happy to see a sober person. "Oh my God. They all came over after the dance and now no one will leave!"

Cat rolled her eyes. "Did you invite them?"

Issa hemmed. "Uh…no…"

"Obviously if you invite people here, they'll come. Everyone's dying to get into my dad's liquor cabinet and hot tub! What are you? A moron?"

A little bit, yeah. Even Issa had to admit it. The scene was out of control. And it was all her fault. Why, oh, why hadn't she told Rake no at the dance itself and come home alone to an empty house? A pint of Ben & Jerry's and rerun episodes of *Gilmore Girls* sounded really good right about now.

"Okay, okay, so it's a bit out of control. We need to get everyone out of here. Right now!"

Cat shrugged and picked up her skirts. "This is your problem. Deal with it. Your Highness." Her tone was smug and sarcastic.

Issa felt the last shred of hope seeping out of her. Even Cat was deserting her now.

"This place is a freaking disaster area. When Dad and Alisha get back, you're dead," Cat yelled from upstairs.

"Cat!" Issa called out. "Come on!"

Cat ignored her and made her way into her room.

A second later, Issa heard a piercing shriek and a girl in a half-undone dress and a guy in his boxers flew out of Cat's room.

"Dude, chill!" the guy yelled to Cat.

"If you don't get the hell out of my house this second, I am calling the police."

That seemed to be enough to the couple. They scurried out the back door, the girl hurriedly pulling her dress up.

Cat stormed down the stairs. "You so owe me."

Issa stood frozen as Cat stalked into the kitchen and turned on the house intercom. She cleared her throat, a loud *squee* noise reverberating through the house. "The police have been called. They will be here in ten minutes to arrest each and every one of you for trespassing."

Issa watched, impressed, as every single activity in the house stopped. Within the next two minutes, a flood of students exited the house like an army of rats running from a tiger.

She breathed a sigh of relief as the house cleared out, then collapsed into a chair in the formerly pristine white living room. She surveyed the damage. Stained carpets. Alcohol pouring out of bottles everywhere. Scraps of clothing all over the floors. And that was just the inside of the house.

Issa felt a torrent of tears rising. What had she done? Not only were Diego and Alisha going to kill her for sneaking her name into the Snow Queen ballot, but Diego would probably sue her for destroying his beautiful house.

How the hell Cat had pulled off these parties for the past few years without getting caught was beyond her. There was literally no way to clean up this place in the next day. She was dead.

She heard Cat's footsteps as she stormed around the house checking for any more unwanted guests. Then she heard the footsteps raging toward the living room. She braced herself. Cat was going to blow up at her, and honestly, she did deserve it.

"What the hell is the matter with you! This is not your house. You can't throw parties here."

Issa held her breath to keep from screaming back. Cat was right. She didn't belong here. And now everyone, including Diego and Alisha, would see that. This would definitely cement the end of Diego and Alisha's engagement.

Of course she would get killed and be grounded for life after that, but it was probably worth it.

"Ever since you came my life has been hell. *Hell!* I hate you! Why don't you just fall off a bridge or something?" Cat continued screaming.

"It's been a total fiesta for me too," Issa mumbled.

"What? What the hell did you say?"

"I said it was a total fiesta for me too!"

Before Issa knew what was happening, Cat was on top of her. She grabbed a handful of Issa's hair and pulled. "You bitch! I hate you! I hate you! Just die!"

"Let go of me! Get off!" Issa struggled to get Cat off her, but the psychopath was surprisingly strong. Issa could feel strands of hair popping off her scalp. "Ow! You're hurting me!"

Cat continued to claw and scratch. "I hate you! I'll kill you!"

Issa reached around, grabbed a handful of Cat's ponytail and yanked.

"Ahhh!"

Cat flew off Issa and landed on the floor, a murderous look in her eyes.

"Stop. Stop right there. Stop." Issa scrambled to her feet on top of the couch, keeping a safe distance between her and Cat.

Cat breathed hard and grabbed a fallen lamp.

Oh God. Issa held up her hands to block her face. This could get ugly.

"If you hate me so much, ask your dad to mot marry my mom!" Issa yelled from around her raised hands.

Crash. Cat dropped the lamp. "You don't think I tried? You don't think I begged and pleaded with him? You don't think I guilt-tripped him about not loving *my* mom anymore?"

Issa lowered her hands. Harsh. That *had* been pretty low of Cat. Guilting Diego by using a dead mother.

"*Papi* said he would have us *both* sent to boarding school if we didn't learn to get along. He said he loved your mother and she loved him and they deserve happiness. They are *not* breaking up."

Issa couldn't help it. She burst into tears. They were so stupid. Why were they so determined to be together when they saw how miserable their children were?

She buried her face in the couch and sobbed, smearing the white leather with her eyeliner. "I wanted my mom and dad to get back together. I just want them together!"

Issa felt a weight on the couch and felt Cat's breath on her arm. "You know that's not going to happen."

Issa sniffed. "It could. If Diego and Alisha broke up, it could. I could have my dad back!"

Cat shook her head. "No, it couldn't. I asked Alisha once. If she had never met *Papi*, and Roy had come back to you guys, would she take him back? She said no way. He'd hurt her too badly and she could never trust him again. Apparently your brother feels the same way too."

Amir was against her too? Who was left now?

Issa rested her head against her arm. So she'd been doing all this for nothing. There was no chance.

The realization slowly settled around her like an ice storm. It was over. Their old life was over.

Alisha and Diego were not going to break up. They would come back with a wedding site picked out and a wedding date set.

And she was dead after they saw this house.

That brought on a fresh round of tears. "I don't want to be here," she sobbed.

Cat sat silently. But then, after a moment, said, "I don't want you here either. But guess what. You and Alisha are here to stay. And in a few weeks, you guys are moving into the house itself. We'll all be under one roof."

A lifetime of fighting with Cat. Issa shuddered. Maybe there was some way for her to graduate early and go to college that moment. She couldn't take one more day of this.

"You're pathetic."

Issa buried her face in the sofa and didn't care how ugly she looked when crying.

"Stop crying. That doesn't do anything. You're still dead when they get home."

Issa practically howled.

"Look, I'll cut you a deal."

Issa looked up, surprised, tears stopping instantly. A deal? Cat wanted to make a deal? She held all the cards. What did Issa possibly have to offer her now?

"We have to learn to deal with each other," Cat said. "Otherwise we're both going to end up at a boarding school somewhere in Siberia. And that will not be cool."

"So?"

"We have to learn to get along. 'Cause I am *not* going to wear a uniform for the rest of my life!"

Issa hesitated. Learn to get along. For real. A real, honest effort. She and Cat were going to be sisters. There was no way out.

"We don't have to be friends or anything, we just have to stay out of each other's way. And you have to tell *Papi* you want your own car because I am *not* sharing my Lotus anymore!"

Issa managed a smile. She was getting tired of the tiny two-seater anyway. Maybe that cute little SUV that was coming out...

"I'll help you clean up this mess. There's this service that handles just this type of thing. I have them on speed dial. Don't you dare tell *Papi* or I'll make sure he hears about this little incident. Got it, *chica?*"

Issa nodded her head. So that was how Cat always cleaned up her messes. Paid someone. If she thought she was going to get away with blackmail, well, she had another thing coming. Two could play the Cat Morena game.

"Um, yeah. I bet Diego'll really believe you had nothing to do with this mess. You have a history of these things, *chica*. So don't try threatening me."

Cat narrowed her eyes. Issa narrowed hers back and was positive Cat was going to jump on her again.

Instead Cat's lips twitched and Issa thought she saw a slightly respectful smile. Who knew? The way to win Cat's respect had been to out-Cat Cat.

"Whatever. Fine. But you have to stop making me look bad to my dad, you have to stop going after guys I like and you have to stop turning people against me."

"But you can't be all psycho-bitch to me either," Issa reminded her.

"I haven't been that in months!"

Issa laughed for real. God, Cat was a piece of work.

"Deal or no deal?" Cat prodded, holding up her cell phone.

"Yeah, fine. Deal." Issa stuck out her hand.

They shook on it and for the first time in a long while, Issa felt relief and like the eighty-five-pound weight had just floated away.

CHAPTER 20

If You Can't Get Rid of the Skeleton In Your Closet, You'd Best Teach It to Dance

Issa stood in the center of the living-room floor, the Snow Queen crown still on her head. Steam vacuums spun around her. The sound of clinking glass could be heard as a trio of maids picked up beer bottles all around the house. A small Russian man touched up the paint chips in the walls with the exact shade of Morena mansion white.

Amazing. So this was how Cat threw her parties and got away with it. Issa was awestruck at the expertise and the speed of the cleaning crowd. Scarcely half an hour after Cat speed-dialed You Wreck It, We Fix It, an army of people had arrived in the driveway in three big white vans. Cat had given rapid directions in Spanish and warned Issa to stay out of their way before disappearing into her room, the only untouched sanctuary in the whole house.

Issa watched as a tiny Mexican woman with a tightly wound braid deftly scooted a white leather couch away from the wall, sprayed carpet cleaner on the soiled spot Issa hadn't even noticed and motioned for the vacuumers to finish up.

How many times had they done this? Issa glanced up at Cat's closed door. No wonder she was so spoiled. She could make any problem go away by throwing money at it. Except one. Cat couldn't get rid of what she thought of as competition for her father's attention. She'd nearly destroyed her high-school career in the process.

"*Senorita?*" The expert cleaning lady was holding a vacuum and standing in front of Issa.

"Sorry. Um, *lo siento.*"

"*De nada.*" The woman smiled and gestured toward the stairs. Issa removed the crown off her head, realizing how stupid she looked, and took a seat.

She sat and watched the army put the house back together. If only her life could be fixed by a cell-phone number. Issa's stomach churned. She and Cat had called a truce, but what next? She continued to hang with the Belles and tried to dissuade them from making Cat miserable? Not possible. She'd sold her soul to the Belles just to win the crown. They would expect her to pay up, they would expect her to join in all of their exploits to humiliate Cat. And the war at home would never end.

The other option wasn't much better.

She gave up her crown and resumed her life of anonymity? Gigi and Ishaan would probably never speak to her again. She wasn't quite ready to go back to a life of social outcastism yet, this time with not a single friend in her corner.

Adam, a voice whispered. She could have him back. He

was waiting for her. He'd made that plenty clear at the dance. They could be a couple again...start the year over.

But thinking of his familiar eyes and sweet smile didn't excite her anymore. She didn't want him. Nor did she want Rake. She felt slimy just thinking of how quickly things with Rake had gotten out of hand. She was not that girl. No guys for a while. She rubbed the sides of her scalp.

"Now what?"

No answer from the heavens. Her identity was something she was going to have to figure out on her own. A hated teen queen or a liked social reject, it was up to her.

"Sucks," Issa said out loud.

"Do you want to see something?"

Issa whirled around.

Cat was sitting at the top of the stairs. Issa could tell she'd been there awhile. Watching her have a mental conversation like a crazy person.

Issa stood up, still a little wary. Hopefully Cat wasn't planning to show Issa her best drop-kick.

"Come up."

Issa followed with a safe distance. Cat was inviting her to her room? Issa would have been more comfortable entering the Osbournes' house shortly after one of their drug scandals.

Cat disappeared behind the Princess sign. "Come on in."

Issa poked her head in and felt like she'd stepped back in time.

Fuzzy pink bedsheets, white curtains, dolls and stuffed animals littering the neatly made bed.

The room looked like it would have belonged to Cat when she was six years old.

Issa glanced at the photographs on the walls. All of Cat and Diego when she was younger. Nothing of Cat as a teenager.

"It's silly," Cat muttered as she caught Issa looking at her photos.

"It's sweet. Very innocent," Issa said, and took a seat gingerly on the bed. Sweet. Innocent. But a little weird.

"*Papi's* idea to keep my room like this. He can't see me grow up."

Was Cat blushing?

"He loves you very much." Issa felt almost envious as she looked around the room. Cat had had a privileged childhood. So unlike her own childhood with Roy and Alisha always struggling over jobs and money.

In the corner, Issa spotted the Barbie Dream House she'd coveted as a six-year-old. And the Barbie pink Mustang parked out front.

"He loves the eight-year-old me. You're lucky, you know, Alisha treats you as an adult, like her equal. I don't know what that's like."

Issa was surprised by Cat's honesty. It was true. Alisha had always treated her as an equal. For as long as she could remember, her parents had referred to her as an adult.

But not Diego. Diego hadn't moved past the tragedy that had taken his wife's life. He still clung to the image of Cat as she had been then. Preserved as a little girl.

And Cat, all she wanted was to show him that she was a grown-up now. The hard partying. The guys. All cries for attention, but she was so afraid of disappointing her father, she hid all her escapades.

A silent rebellion.

Here the whole time Issa had thought Cat acted the way she did because she could and did her best to hide it from her father. But it seemed to be that all she'd wanted was for Diego to notice.

She needed a mother.

She needed Alisha.

The realization nearly toppled Issa. Alisha was exactly what Cat needed. Someone who saw her as an equal. Someone who helped her plan for the future and trusted her to act as an adult. And Issa needed Diego. Someone to show her that she was still someone's daughter, not a mother. She still needed to be taken care of sometimes. In some demented way, this whole scenario was fitting half people into wholes.

"What do you think?" Cat was gesturing toward a paint canvas.

Issa let her eyes focus on the easel. *Oh my God.*

It was a portrait of the four of them. When had they ever taken a picture together?

Issa recognized the pose she and Alisha were in. They had been at a haunted house the previous year. Alisha was pulling Issa tightly into her shoulder. Alisha's eyes were sparkling and Issa was grinning.

Cat and Diego were in an old-school pose, Cat sitting in a high-backed chair with Diego's hand on her shoulder.

Cat had merged a photograph of her and Diego with a photo of Issa and Alisha and painted it.

Issa couldn't even speak. There it was. The four of them immortalized as a family. Cat had accepted it first and made the theory of the four of them a reality.

"I did it for class. You mom's been helping me. I wanted, to, uh, hang it in the living room. You know, after you guys move in."

Issa turned to face Cat, a flood of emotions surging through her: understanding, realization and respect.

After they moved in. Cat hadn't even thought for a second that this wedding wouldn't take place. She was ready for her new family.

The Morena-Mazumder family was being born. Diego and Alisha understood it. Even Cat understood it. It was time for Issa to understand it. It was time for Issa to embrace her new life and stop fighting.

"It's awesome." Issa gestured toward the painting. "I can never do anything like it. Your dad will love it. And, uh, so...so do I."

Cat smiled.

Issa strode through the hallways to the athletes' wing early Monday morning. She'd made some frank decisions and she knew she had to do some things before she chickened out.

"Jenni!" she called as the tall, muscular blond girl came into view.

The frown on Jenni's face didn't disappear as Issa approached. "What do you want?"

Issa knew Jenni was plenty annoyed with her. Going into the voting on Friday morning, there was supposed to be only one name on the ballot, Jenni Wilson, along with a write-in candidate.

Instead there had been two names: Isabelle Mazumder and Jenni Wilson. Isabelle had won by a landslide without even giving Jenni's jock buddies any time to do any campaigning for the popular athlete.

"I need to give you something."

Jenni, already in her shoulder pads and lacrosse cleats, didn't look impressed. "What? A headache? Look, I hate girls like you. You act all nice, but actually you're scheming and plotting. I didn't think you were like them, but you are. So get out of my way. Or I'll beat your ass."

Issa took a deep breath. She had been acting like "one of them." But that was about to change.

"I'm really sorry. This belongs to you." Issa pulled the glistening Snow Queen crown out of her messenger bag. "I cheated to get it and that was stupid. It's yours."

Jenni's eyes were on the crown. Suddenly she didn't look like a terrifying linebacker, but instead, an excited teenage girl.

"That's lame," Jenni said unconvincingly. "The night's over. What do I want with that stupid crown now?"

Issa tried to hide her smile. "I know I can't give you back that night. It should have been you onstage. And you in the spotlight dancing with your boyfriend."

"Jake."

"Jake?"

"The guy I like."

"Yeah, it should have been you and Jake." Issa held out the crown. "Please take it."

"Seriously?"

"Totally. Should I put it on you?"

Jenni ducked her six-foot-tall frame down and Issa set the crown on her head.

"Gorgeous."

She made quite the sight in a lacrosse uniform and a silver tiara, but the smile on her face made her the most beautiful girl in the stinky hallway.

"Wow. Cool." Jenni didn't take her eyes off herself in her locker mirror.

"It's perfect on you." Issa grinned. Doing the right thing felt really good. "You should go show Jake right now."

Jenni grinned. "Yeah. Thanks. I think I will."

"Nice." A familiar voice sounded amused.

Issa spun around. Ishaan and Gigi were both smiling as they leaned a few feet away. Gigi's arms were wrapped tightly around Ishaan's waist, her head resting on his chest.

Issa swallowed. They were together. There was no doubt in her mind as Ishaan gently tucked a strand of hair behind Gigi's hear and kissed her forehead.

"That's the Issa we know." Gigi couldn't stop smiling. "Back to normal now? Is Isabelle dead?"

Issa didn't know whether to laugh or cry. What was normal? Her best friends were talking to her again, but…they were dating. They had moved on without her. Ishaan had decided to take a chance on Gigi and he seemed happy. Really happy. What had become of his mystery woman? Issa wondered.

"I'm really sorry for—I just didn't know where I belonged," Issa said lamely.

Gigi pulled away from Ishaan. "Don't be a moron. You belong with us."

Issa swallowed back tears as her friends enveloped her in a hug. This felt right. Finally, things were as they were supposed to be.

When she pulled away, she couldn't help feeling a prick of jealousy as she noticed Ishaan and Gigi gazing into each other's eyes. She couldn't understand if the jealousy was because she was alone, or because she had missed out on a part of her friends' lives. A huge part of their lives.

Or could it be because of the sneaking suspicion that she had fallen for Ishaan without even realizing it?

And now it was too late.

"I have to run. Cheerleading practice." Gigi giggled. "Iz, call me later, okay?"

Issa nodded and averted her eyes as Gigi pecked Ishaan on the lips.

"See ya, Iz!"

Issa raised her hand in a goodbye.

Ishaan turned his head to watch Gigi walk away and when he faced Issa again, he was smiling.

"You guys seem really happy." Issa suddenly felt self-conscious. She had no idea how to act around Ishaan and Gigi now. She had a miserable feeling that whenever the three of them hung out from then on, she would be the third wheel.

"I'm happy. I hope she is," Ishaan said as he twirled his locker combination. "She asked me if I wanted to go to the dance, and I figured—"

"You don't have to explain to me," Issa said, wondering why he felt the need to do so. "I mean, I was so out of my mind I probably wouldn't have noticed if you two had gotten hitched."

Ishaan laughed.

"So, um." Issa knew she shouldn't have even thought of asking, but the question had been nagging her at for months. "What happened to your mystery woman?"

"Mystery woman?" Ishaan piled his AP Physics book on top of his AP Chemistry and AP Biology books.

"Remember that day you gave me a ride? You told me you didn't want to date Gigi because there was someone else. What happened to her?"

Ishaan avoided her eyes as he slammed his locker shut. "She moved on."

Gigi's words came back to Issa again. *He's so totally in love with you.* "On to what? Or on to who?"

"Another guy. Another life. She very obviously wasn't interested in me."

Issa had a feeling she understood exactly the look Ishaan gave her. He was always able to tell what she was thinking. Maybe she was picking up his talent.

"Her loss, then," Issa said softly. "She wasn't ready for you yet."

Ishaan gave her a sad smile. "I guess not."

CHAPTER 21

How on Earth Do You Salsa in a Sari?

ROY Bradley paced in front of the couch where Issa sat. After so long, she was in their old house in Detroit. She felt waves of nostalgia washing over her, remembering all the late-night dinner and movie sessions and game nights their family had shared in that very room.

"A seaside wedding in December?"

Issa nodded. "Friday in the Hamptons. Diego rented a place there for the week. Mom let me come up. She finally thinks it's healthy for me to see you again."

"And your brother?"

"He won't see you."

Roy sighed. "I figured."

"I'm sorry, Dad. I thought for sure I would be able to break up Mom and Diego. I just—" Issa bit her lip. She didn't want to tell him that maybe her plan hadn't been the best idea.

"So she's really doing it. She's marrying that guy." Roy

finally sat down and buried his face in his hands. "I thought she would come back to me. I really did."

Issa had thought so too. But Alisha had stuck by Diego through everything. They really did love each other. And Issa was slowly getting used to the idea.

"You know, you and I can still be a family."

Issa glanced at her father.

"If you can't deal with staying in New Joliet with the Morenas, you can always move here with me. I mean, this place is huge enough for five people and I'm here all alone...."

Issa knew what her dad was thinking. If she refused to live at the Morenas maybe Alisha would follow.

She frowned. That was playing dirty and she wouldn't put Alisha in that situation. Not anymore. She was surprised her father would be willing to use her to get to Alisha.

Maybe Roy wasn't as mature and as grown-up as he claimed.

Issa shook her head, wanting to let him down gently. He was still her father. Immature or not. "I don't think so. I mean, two months ago, I totally would have tried it, but you know, things have changed."

"Changed?"

"Yeah. Cat and I called a truce and Mom really seems happy there."

"She does, huh?"

"Yeah."

"Okay." Roy reached out and put an arm around Issa. "If you say so. But I don't know if I'm going to give up."

Issa closed her eyes and rested her chin on her father's shoulder. He'd made a mistake and now he had to pay the price. He had to let go of Alisha. But that was something he had to figure out on his own. Like she'd had to.

"I love you, Dad."

"You too, kid. Friday, huh?"

"Friday. Just a little ceremony. Just the immediate family and a priest."

"Wow."

They sat there like that for a long time before Issa disentangled herself to catch the last train back to New Joliet.

Friday morning rolled around and Issa stood in front of the full-length mirror in one of the guest rooms in the rented villa.

Horrified her mother wasn't wearing a traditional sari to get married, Issa had insisted on wearing one herself. There had to be at least one Hindu tradition at this very non-Hindu wedding. It was a very basic ceremony, just vow exchanges, no fancy Indian walking around the fire business. No sari necessary. But she'd felt like doing something, anything to represent who she and Alisha were. So here she was, draped in twelve feet of thick silk cloth.

When Cat had seen Alisha wrapping one of her old saris around Issa, she'd demanded that she get to wear one, as well.

Issa could barely move, much less walk in a straight line. Cat had danced in half an hour prior to show off her pale pink sari and let them know Diego and Amir were in their suits and ready to roll.

Unfair. Cat was managing so well in hers and she wasn't even Indian.

Alisha, in a gorgeous pale blue tea-length gown, was applying a coat of mascara in the bathroom mirror. "You look great," she commented as she replaced her makeup. "I can't believe how different you look in a sari."

Issa fingered the thick midnight-blue cloth draped elaborately around her. "Me neither."

She liked what she saw. The heavy kohl eyeliner on her eyes, the lush lips, the silvery *bindi* on her forehead. But she still couldn't take a single normal-sized step.

"You look like my mother."

Issa glanced up from the armful of bangles she was arranging, alarmed.

Alisha laughed at her expression. "In a good way. She was a major babe when she was young."

"Uh-huh." Issa had never heard Alisha refer to her mother as a "major babe" before.

"Ready?"

Issa hesitated. No. She wasn't. Probably she never would be. She felt her eyes filling with tears. She would have to share Alisha from this day forward.

"I love you, Mom."

Alisha set down the bouquet of tulips she was sniffing. "Baby, I love you too. I really need you and me to stay best friends. We Mazumders need to stick together. Deal?"

Issa managed a smile. "Deal."

"And I'm sorry I kept you from your father. I know you wanted us together, but I'm glad you finally saw that we've been over for a while now."

If only she knew... "Thanks, Mom."

Mother hugged daughter and they walked down the stairs arm in arm where Diego, Amir and Cat were waiting.

"Baby sis. Look at you," Amir murmured. College in California had done him good. He seemed to have grown an inch and was even more handsome than before he'd left. His hazel eyes twinkled as she took his arm. They followed Diego and Alisha, who walked hand in hand to the gazebo.

Issa grinned as she took her baby sari steps. "I can't breathe!"

"You look like Mom's mom," Amir whispered.

Issa glanced at him. "You've seen her?"

"Pictures. Maybe we'll see them in person one day. They'd be glad to meet you."

Issa doubted they would ever meet their grandparents. Alisha had made it very clear they had wanted nothing to do with her ever again after they'd found out about her and Roy. And now if they found out she'd married a Cuban guy with a kid, they would disown her again for good.

But then Issa had changed her mind about wanting nothing to do with Cat either...maybe...

"What're you guys whispering about? Walk faster!" Cat ordered from behind them.

Issa stifled a laugh. Like it or not, this was her family now. Crazy Cat Morena and her clueless father.

The ceremony happened too quickly. Diego and Alisha, with lowered eyes, said their vows in hushed tones. Choppy gray waves washed against the shore, overlooked by the gazebo.

Issa heard Amir intake a sharp breath of air as the minister asked Alisha if she took Diego till death did her part.

Issa counted the seconds. Would her mother go through with it? Was Amir hoping she wouldn't?

She glanced at her brother. His eyes were glistening with tears. Happiness? Sadness?

"I do. Forever," Alisha whispered.

Diego pressed his lips against Alisha's and Issa didn't feel the urge to turn away. It was done. Nothing more she could do now. Her eyes met Cat's. Both girls stared warily at each other.

They weren't friends by a long shot. Maybe they never would be, but Issa had a feeling that each of them had a pretty good idea who the other was and why they were the way they were.

Maybe this could work.

Maybe.

The ceremony ended as beautifully as it had begun. The five of them entered the ballroom in their rented house followed by a champagne toast for the parents and slices of cake for all.

As the salsa band Diego had hired started up a rendition of "Bailamos," Diego twirled Alisha expertly across the floor and dipped her. Issa smiled. She hadn't seen that smile on her mother's face in a while. The smile looked an awful lot like the one in the photograph with Roy.

"All right. Salsa, baby!" Cat jumped up, swigging the last of the champagne from Diego's glass and shooting Issa a warning look when Issa glanced at her disapprovingly. Cat gracefully hit the dance floor as if she'd been salsa-ing in the bulky sari her whole life.

Issa shook her head. Cat was still Cat. Diego really needed to open his eyes one of these days.

"How're you holding up?" Amir asked quietly. He checked his cell phone and replaced it in his pocket.

"Okay." Issa picked at her remaining slice of cake. It was so good to have him back. An ally. Maybe he'd stay awhile. There was so much to tell him. He would be horrified by the stunts she'd pulled, but proud at how she'd handled herself at the end.

"I want you to know something. I dropped out of school."

"What?" Issa set down her fork. Alisha was going to kill him but she didn't care. He was going to stay for good. They were going to have so much fun.

"Now that I know Mom is okay, well, there are things I need to do."

Issa's heart sank. This didn't sound like sticking around to her. "Like?"

"I need to do something for this country."

"Like volunteering?"

Amir laughed and hugged her. "You're so cute. Something like that. Don't tell Mom yet."

"I wouldn't even know *what* to tell her."

Amir just grinned. "Don't worry about it. Let's just enjoy the day."

Issa shook her head.

Where did he get these ideas from? The previous year he'd been all set to join the peace corps, but a scholarship from UCLA had lured him to California.

"Okay, but—"

"Come on, you two. Let's salsa!" Cat called.

"Go," Amir prodded.

She would think about this later. She would drag the details out of him that night when they stayed up till dawn and caught up on all the news.

"You come too!" Issa grabbed his hand and dragged him with her.

As the explosive beat continued, Issa picked up her sari at the waist and tried to move her feet. Her sandals just wound up getting tangled and she swore her sari was going to fall off, exposing the designer jeans she'd slipped on underneath just in case of such an emergency.

A few yards away, Cat was swiveling her hips to the beat, Amir barely moving.

"Too much hip movement for me." Amir tried to back away.

Cat grabbed his arms and pulled him to her. "You're doing great."

Did she really have to flirt with *everyone?* Issa frowned as Cat dragged Amir closer to her. Amir glanced at Issa nervously.

Issa shuffled closer to them and managed to scoot between them. There was no way in hell she was letting Cat Morena flirt with her *brother.*

Amir winked. "I think I'll just watch for a while. You babes are too advanced for an old guy like me."

"Amir! How the hell do I salsa in a sari?" Issa called after him.

"It's not too hard." Cat caught a hold of Issa's flailing arms. "I'll show you."

Issa swung her hips in figure eights, imitating Cat. Just when she thought she'd gotten it, she lost her balance.

"I suck!" Issa said, frustrated again as her sandal threatened to slip off.

"Yeah, you do." Cat stopped dancing.

"Thanks a lot."

"I was going to say, you do suck, but when has that ever stopped you?"

"Gee, thanks."

"No prob."

As Issa watched her new sister dance next to her, she wondered if she and Cat would be able to peacefully salsa into the future in their saris.

Maybe, and maybe not. But they would have a hell of a time trying.

KIMANI
tru
™

Sometimes the right person
is closer than you think.

Monica McKayhan
indigo summer

Fifteen-year-old Indigo Summer's world finally
seems to be going in the right direction. The star
of the school basketball team has asked her out,
and she makes the high school dance squad all in
one week. But when her perfect world suddenly falls
apart, Indigo finds herself turning to her best friend,
Marcus Carter. The problem is now that Indigo
realizes what a great guy Marcus really is,
so does someone else.

"An engaging and compelling read."
—Romantic Times BOOKreviews
on *From Here to Forever*

Available the first week of February, wherever books are sold.

www.kimanipress.com   KPMM7560207TR

Essence Bestselling Author

MONICA McKAYHAN

TROUBLE FOLLOWS

An INDIGO Novel

Indigo Summer seems to have everything she wants, including Marcus, her hot boyfriend and Jade, her best friend. But trouble soon follows when Jade starts making poor decisions and Marcus finds himself fighting to prove his innocence. Indigo's feeling the pressure, and it's time to show everyone—including herself—that she's made of strong stuff.

"This is McKayhan's debut title, but I'm hoping it will not be her last. Her writing was crisp and strong…"
—*Rawsistaz Reviewers* on *As Real as it Gets*

Available the first week of December wherever books are sold.

www.KimaniTRU.com   KPMM0871207TR